PENGUIN BOOKS

Odd One Out

Monica McInerney is the author of five best-selling novels, *Family Baggage*, *The Alphabet Sisters*, *Spin the Bottle*, *Upside Down Inside Out* and *A Taste for It*, published internationally and in translation. Monica grew up in a family of seven children in the Clare Valley wine region of South Australia, where her father was the railway stationmaster. She has worked in book publishing, arts marketing, children's television and the music industry, and lived in many parts of Australia and in Ireland and England. She and her Irish husband currently live in Dublin, where she is working on her next novel.

For more information please visit
www.monicamcinerney.com

Praise for Monica McInerney

'McInerney is a dab hand at getting her characters exactly right. They are utterly believable, often lovable and familiar'
West Australian

'Her books are for handbags and airports, traffic jams, railway stations and bus stops. They make us forget the irritating details of the day . . . Warmly written, kindly and empathetic'
Sydney Morning Herald

'With every book, Monica McInerney becomes more skilled at juggling plot complexities and giving depth to her characters . . . Perfect weekend reading'
Marie Claire

'Disarmingly funny . . . McInerney's story and plot resonates with a Maeve Binchy kind of generosity of spirit . . . Compassionate, clever and sometimes poignant'
The Age

'Vivid characterizations and sharply honed dialogue . . . McInerney brings humour and insight to issues of sibling rivalry, family secrecy, and romantic betrayal'
Boston Globe

'A charming and exciting family drama, full of surprises'
Evening Herald, Ireland

MONICA McINERNEY

Odd One Out

PENGUIN GROUP (AUSTRALIA)
Published in association with Books Alive 2006.
Books Alive is an Australian Government initiative
developed through the Australia Council for the Arts,
the Australian Government's arts funding and advisory body.

PENGUIN BOOKS

Published by the Penguin Group
Penguin Group (Australia)
250 Camberwell Road, Camberwell, Victoria 3124, Australia
(a division of Pearson Australia Group Pty Ltd)
Penguin Group (USA) Inc.
375 Hudson Street, New York, New York 10014, USA
Penguin Group (Canada)
90 Eglinton Avenue East, Suite 700, Toronto ON M4P 2Y3, Canada
(a division of Pearson Penguin Canada Inc.)
Penguin Books Ltd
80 Strand, London WC2R 0RL, England
Penguin Ireland
25 St Stephen's Green, Dublin 2, Ireland
(a division of Penguin Books Ltd)
11 Community Centre, Panchsheel Park, New Delhi – 110 017, India
Penguin Group (NZ)
Cnr Airborne and Rosedale Roads, Albany, Auckland, New Zealand
(a division of Pearson New Zealand Ltd)
Penguin Books (South Africa) (Pty) Ltd
24 Sturdee Avenue, Rosebank, Johannesburg 2196, South Africa

Penguin Books Ltd, Registered Offices: 80 Strand, London WC2R 0RL, England

First published by Penguin Group (Australia), 2006

1 3 5 7 9 10 8 6 4 2

Copyright © Monica McInerney 2006

Design and illustration by Cathy Larsen © Penguin Group (Australia)
Author photograph by David Sievers
Typeset in Sabon by Post Pre-press Group, Brisbane, Queensland
Printed and bound in Australia by McPherson's Printing Group, Maryborough, Victoria

National Library of Australia
Cataloguing-in-Publication data:

McInerney, Monica.
Odd one out.
ISBN-13: 978 0 14300 544 5.
ISBN-10: 0 14300 544 8.
I. Title.

A823.4

www.penguin.com.au

CHAPTER ONE

Though Sylvie Devereaux didn't realise it at the time, her life began to change at exactly five minutes past seven on the evening of her sister Vanessa's second wedding.

The instigator was her Great-Aunt Mill. 'Mill-as-in-short-for-Millicent,' as she always introduced herself. Great-Aunt Foot-in-Mouth, the rest of the family privately called her.

It had been a hectic day for the Devereaux family. As the Sydney society pages would report the following morning: *Two artistic dynasties came together yesterday with the union of fashion designer Vanessa Devereaux and actor Jared Rowe. A who's who of the Sydney art scene was in attendance, including the bride's mother, the celebrated artist Fidelma Devereaux, the bride's sister and bridesmaid, jewellery designer Cleo Devereaux, and her brother Sebastian Devereaux, winner of this year's Green Room Award for outstanding achievement in lighting design. Vanessa, a rising star in the Sydney fashion scene, designed her own dress, a daring and colourful interpretation of the classic Grecian shift style . . .* There would be no mention of Sylvie.

The reception was taking place in the city's most talked about harbourside restaurant. Dinner was served by waiters who looked like models. Rock oysters to begin. Pan-fried sole with truffle shavings and porcini mushrooms on a bed of baby spinach for main course. A concoction of summer berries in an amusement of toffee for dessert.

Sitting one row away from the main bridal table, Sylvie was catching her breath. She'd been on the run all day. Checking details with the celebrant, the photographer, the caterer, the musicians. Fetching the flowers. Returning the flowers when Vanessa wasn't happy with them. Moving furniture in the hotel suite at Vanessa's insistence. Moving it back at the photographer's insistence. Driving to the family home to fetch a handbag her mother had left behind. Stopping on the way at her mother and sisters' studio to collect a necklace Cleo had forgotten. Going back to the studio and the house again for more handbags and necklaces when they changed their minds. Keeping everyone fed and hydrated, dialling room service so many times she was on first-name terms with the receptionist.

She'd had fifteen minutes to race home again, do her own makeup and try to style her short curly hair. One minute to lament her ordinary brown eyes and freckled skin, so different from her sisters' blue-eyed classic features. Five minutes to change into her wedding outfit. A normal outfit, not a bridesmaid's dress. Vanessa had asked Cleo to be bridesmaid, again. 'It's good for both our profiles, Sylvie. You understand,' Vanessa said. Sylvie said that of course she did, and hoped her smile hid her hurt. She'd secretly hoped this time it was her turn. Or that Vanessa would have two bridesmaids. When she tentatively suggested this, Vanessa explained it was more fashionable these days to have one.

In her room, Sylvie thought her outfit looked lovely, a green silk dress and matching jacket, green high-heeled shoes and glass earrings. At only five foot two, she'd learnt to avoid complicated patterns or fussy designs. 'You've come as an elf, how sweet,' was all Cleo said. Her mother was too busy directing the hairdresser to pin up her long hair in a particular way to notice Sylvie's outfit. She just gave her a vague wave and said she looked charming. She'd said the same thing about Sylvie's working clothes of jeans and T-shirt that morning. Vanessa didn't say anything. She was too busy posing for photographs. Sylvie's only hope for a compliment was from her big brother, Sebastian, her closest ally in the family. As a child,

Sylvie had secretly thought of him as her separated twin, cheerfully ignoring the seven-year age difference. They were very alike in appearance even now. Unfortunately, his flight from Melbourne had been delayed so many times it looked like the most he'd see of the wedding was the cutting of the cake.

He finally arrived at the reception at seven p.m. Sylvie's spirits lifted as he came through the garlanded door. Although they'd spoken on the phone now and again, it was the first time they'd seen each other in ten months. He was out of his normal jeans and casual shirts, dressed in a dark-blue suit, a red tie, his unruly hair tamed into a more sober style than usual. Short for a man, only five foot six, he was often mistaken for a mid-twenties student, not the thirty-six-year-old success story he was. 'It's my boyish charm, not my height,' he always said.

Sylvie had heard Vanessa on the phone, unsubtly telling him he needed to dress up for the occasion. 'A lot of my clients will be here, Sebastian. I want to make the right impression. Not like last time.' He'd come straight from a country film set to her first wedding, dirt still on his shoes. She hadn't spoken to him for weeks. 'I can see her point,' he'd said to Sylvie. 'It's my fault the marriage failed. If I'd worn a suit they'd be celebrating their fifth anniversary about now.' When he'd heard the decorative theme of this wedding was water, he'd told Sylvie he was thinking about coming in a wetsuit.

Sylvie was waving to get his attention when she heard her name being called. Shouted, in fact. It was Great-Aunt Mill, across the room at the elderly-members-of-the-family table. In her early seventies, short and plump, she was dressed in a red dress with a wide cream collar. She had pinned her white hair into a lopsided bun, adding a jaunty red bow to the back. The whole effect was unfortunately like a giant jelly cake.

Sylvie excused herself to her neighbour (an old school friend of Vanessa's who'd spent the past hour talking about his stock portfolio) and made her way through the round, beautifully decorated tables. Each blue and white flower arrangement had cost more than Sylvie's dress. She'd barely sat down before Great-Aunt Mill took her hand.

'You're not to worry, little Sylvie.'

'About what, Aunt Mill?'

'About being left on the shelf.'

'But I'm not worried.'

'Of course you are. Any girl would be on a day like today. You're probably thinking, "It's not fair. One of my sisters is long married, the other has been married twice. That's our family's share of weddings all used up." Unless Sebastian surprises us, of course, but they don't tend to marry, his sort of people, do they? They're not allowed to, are they? We all guessed even when he was a young boy, you know. Always putting on those little plays and asking for dance lessons. Is he here yet? I haven't seen him. But it's not him I'm concerned about, it's you. "I've missed out," you're thinking. "I'm going to be single for life."'

'I wasn't, really.'

Mill patted Sylvie's hand. 'It can be hard being the youngest one, I know. My youngest sister, Letitia, that's your other great-aunt, was never happy. Couldn't seem to find her place in the world. You look like her, you know. Small. That same springy hair. Same big smile too. You might be taking after her in life, as well. Not that she lived long. Died aged twenty-four, God rest her soul. Measles. Or was it chicken pox? Something spotty anyway.'

'I'm nearly out of my twenties, Mill. I should be okay. And I'm fit as a fiddle.'

'Of course you are. Anyone can see that. You've got your grandfather's farming genes in you. Fine agricultural bloodstock. Strong and sturdy, like a little ox.' Aunt Mill leaned in close enough for Sylvie to get a quick blast of sherry-scented breath. 'Which is why I have a proposition for you.'

'To sell me as breeding stock?'

Aunt Mill gave a burst of laughter. 'How funny. Now, you've been working around Sydney as a pimp for the past few years, your mother tells me.'

'A temp, Mill.'

'A tip? What about?'

'Temp. I'm a temp. It's short for temporary secretary.'

'Nothing to be ashamed about. It can't be easy to find permanent work these days. And not everyone gets given a special talent like your mother did. And your sisters. And your brother. Your father too, though I probably shouldn't mention him on a happy day like today. He's not here, I suppose? No, of course he isn't. As I was saying, the rest of us are the worker bees. I was a housekeeper all my life, as you know, and it never did me any harm. Where is it you said you're working?'

Sylvie was tempted to say a side street in Kings Cross. 'I'm working back at the studio again, with Mum and Vanessa and Cleo. Doing their admin.' They'd called her in a panic six months previously, when their regular PA walked out in a huff on the eve of an exhibition opening. Sylvie had been there since. Apart from answering the phone, typing letters, sending orders, updating databases and doing filing, she also ran errands, booked restaurants, sent flowers and kept an eye on their supplies of herbal tea, spring water, rice cakes, pecans, blueberries, vitamin tablets and eye gel.

'A family affair. Oh, good, so you've had some experience.'

'Of what?'

'Working for family.'

The squeal of the microphone interrupted. The speeches were due to start. Sylvie was about to whisper to Mill that she might like to turn her chair around when the old woman put her hand on her arm and gave it a surprisingly tight squeeze. 'I've been watching you all day. Busy as a bee. Grace under pressure. I do believe you're the perfect candidate.'

'I am? For what?'

The best man clinked his glass. The room fell silent. All eyes were turned towards the top table. Which meant that all ninety-five people in the room, including Sylvie's mother, her mother's boyfriend, her three siblings, two brothers-in-law, five well-known Sydney artists, two critics, three gallery owners and sixty members of the Devereaux family's social circle not only clearly heard but also saw Great-Aunt Mill lean over and shout her idea.

'I'm offering you a job as my companion, Sylvie. We can be two old maids together.'

CHAPTER TWO

'So did you accept? It's certainly the offer of a lifetime.'

'I gracefully declined but I said you'd be more than happy to take up the position.'

Sebastian laughed. 'Poor Sylvie. You should have seen your face.'

'I didn't need to see it. I could feel it. And I could see everyone else's faces. Hear them laughing.'

'Not all of them.'

'Don't try and gloss over it, Seb. Everyone heard. Everyone in the room. Everyone in Sydney.'

'Only the inner suburbs. Spin, Sylvie.'

She obeyed, executing a graceful turn. Sebastian had appeared out of nowhere on to the dance floor one song previously, rescuing her from the overly sweaty hands of her dinner partner. 'Excuse me cutting in. I haven't seen my little sister all night.'

'So where is this pad of yours and Mill's?'

'Mum didn't tell you? Her old boss Vincent left her his house, contents and all. It's a two-storey terrace in Surry Hills. She moved in last month.'

Sebastian gave a low whistle. 'That's what I call being a housekeeper. Get it, Sylvie? Housekeeper, keeper of the house?'

'Got it, Seb.'

Sylvie had only met Vincent once, when Great-Aunt Mill brought him to a family gathering. A beetle-browed, slightly stooped man, he had glowered at them all for an hour and then left in a taxi. He'd once been a well-known musician and composer, apparently. Jazz, Sylvie thought. Or was it blues? He'd died of a heart attack several months earlier. Mill had rung and told the family about his death, and her inheritance, sounding surprisingly chipper, Fidelma reported. 'No wonder,' Vanessa had said sniffily. 'Those terrace houses are worth a fortune. I'd be sounding quite chipper myself.'

'She must have been more than his cook and cleaner all those years,' Cleo had said, disgusted. 'I think it's appalling.'

'At least you got your embarrassing Mill moment out of the way early,' Sebastian said as they finished a complicated move. 'Now you can relax. Enjoy yourself.'

'Knowing everyone thinks I'm an old maid?'

'They heard your batty old relative ask you a batty

old question. They didn't see you fall on your knees in gratitude and accept. *That* would have been truly embarrassing. For me, at least. Not to mention the rest of your family.'

Their next turn around the dance floor gave Sylvie the perfect view of the rest of her family. Her mother was holding court at the head table. Fidelma had switched seamlessly from her earlier modest mother-of-the-bride role back to Fidelma Devereaux the famous artist, all dramatic gestures and fluttering eyelashes. Sylvie could almost hear her trying to find the exact word to describe a colour or idea she hoped to express in her work. Beside Fidelma was her latest boyfriend, Ray, a not-so-successful artist, poised like a gundog, ready as always to fetch Fidelma a drink, a cigarette, a more comfortable chair.

Vanessa and her new husband were waltzing cheek-to-cheek five couples away. Vanessa's azure blue dress caught the light, with its shimmers, sparkles and elegant lines. Her long blonde hair was a beautiful contrast against it. The photographer was trailing behind them, taking action shots.

Her other sister Cleo and her lawyer husband were standing by the bar. Cleo had her hand extended show-ing a dramatic ring to its greatest advantage. She was her own best advertisement, her handcrafted silver jewellery adorning her fingers, wrist and neck, several glittering hairpins in her blonde curls. Sylvie had already heard her make two appointments to discuss future orders.

'Dip, Sylvie.'

She dipped. Sebastian had taught her to dance when she was a child, just a few months before he and their father left the family home and moved to Melbourne. He'd made a point of giving her refresher lessons every year when he came to Sydney to stay, hearing all her news at the same time. There was plenty to catch up on today. He'd had the busiest year of his career, designing the lighting for three films and two plays. Even this trip was a brief one. He was going back to Melbourne early the next day.

The music changed from the fast salsa beat to a waltz. 'Here's our chance,' he said. 'Music to talk by. Before we start, Dad says hello, by the way.'

'Does he?'

'Don't be like that.'

'Like what?'

'You've gone stiff as a board. Not good for our dancing style.'

'Please say hello back to him.'

'Such warmth and enthusiasm.'

'It's hard to think of anything else to say to him.' Sylvie didn't understand these new attempts by Sebastian to pass on messages from their long-estranged father. She actually wondered whether they were coming from their father at all. 'It's different for us, Seb. Harder.'

'Of course it is. You poor things. I forget.'

'Don't be cross.'

'I'm not cross. Really. Let's talk about you instead. I want a full update.'

'You first. I haven't seen you in months.'

'In a nutshell? Work, great. House, great. Social life, great. Your turn.'

'Social life great? You've met someone?'

'I'm not here to talk about me.'

'You have! Who is he? Where?'

'Someone. In Melbourne.'

'You can't leave it at that.'

'I'm older than you. I can do as I please. Your turn. Start with work. Please tell me you're not still at Union Street.' It was the family's shorthand name for the studio, a converted warehouse in the east inner city. Fidelma, Vanessa and Cleo had recently started calling it Avalon. The name had come to Fidelma in a dream.

'I'm still at Union Street.'

'You promised me you were going to leave. Work anywhere but there.'

'I did leave. Then I came back.' She read his expression. 'I had to, Seb. They needed me. Mum rang me in an absolute panic.'

'Which is why you're back living at home too?'

Back in the family house at Rushcutters Bay, back in

her old bedroom. She was even sleeping in her old bed. 'I know I said I'd never go back, but my flatmate was moving to Brisbane and when Mum rang . . .'

'And said that it was all over between her and Ray yet again and she couldn't bear another night in the house on her own, you couldn't say no?'

'It wasn't like that.' It had been exactly like that.

'And friends? Or have you cast them out of your life as well?'

'I've plenty of friends,' she said, stung. It was true. She had friends from the arts course she'd started at Sydney University as a nineteen-year-old, ten years ago now. People she'd met in student jobs in wine bars and coffee shops. Other temps from the executive agency she'd been with for six years. Everyone was so busy these days, though, getting married or starting to have babies. Settling down. She was the only single one among her group these days.

'So your love life is hectic and fulfilling too?'

She was glad the dance steps meant she could avoid eye contact for a moment. Her love life was like the Sahara. 'Nothing since David.'

'Evil David? That was months ago. No one since? Have you been out with anyone? Asked friends to set you up? Advertised your wares?'

'No, no, no and no. And if I ever asked you those questions you'd tell me to mind my own business.'

'True. Spin.' They spun. 'Have you had a break since I saw you last? One of those old-fashioned things called a holiday?'

'No,' she said simply.

'Sylvie, go to the kitchen and get two spoons, would you?'

'Why?'

'I've arrived in the nick of time. Things are worse for you than I thought. We're going to dig you a tunnel out of here, through the dance floor. I'm thinking *The Great Escape*. Or am I thinking *Chicken Run*? Whichever it is, you need freedom. A new start. Liberty and justice.'

'You're quoting from a play now, aren't you?'

He grinned. 'Just the liberty and justice line, yes. I blame myself. I've neglected you this year.'

'You haven't. And I don't need rescuing. I like being busy.'

'You've gone beyond busy. I can see it just looking at you. You've got "I am stressed" written in block letters on your forehead.'

She rubbed at her forehead without thinking. 'We've had a lot on this year. Three exhibitions. Cleo's new line of jewellery. Vanessa's export orders.'

'So presumably they haven't had holidays either?'

Fidelma had been away to her house on the coast most weekends the past year. Cleo had been to Paris twice. Vanessa had been to Vietnam and Hong Kong. In search of inspiration, they'd said each time.

'You don't have to answer, I can see it on your face,' he said. 'And you kept the home fires burning each time? The office lights ablaze?'

'There was a lot to do. And I wanted to do it properly.'

'And are they paying you properly?'

'As much as they can. Most of the profits go straight back into the business.'

'Straight back into their holiday funds, you mean. Sylvie, why do you keep falling for this? Any time you try to get away, Mum reels you back in. As for Heckle and Jeckle –'

She secretly loved it when Sebastian called Vanessa and Cleo by their childhood nicknames. Especially when he did it to their faces.

He wasn't laughing. 'I'm serious, Sylvie. They're not good to you or for you. You have to get away from them.' He led her skilfully in a sudden complicated dance move. 'I couldn't do it when you were a kid, but I can do it now. I'm airlifting you out of here. Kidnapping you. You're coming to live in Melbourne with me.'

'Really? Great. Let me go and get my bag.'

'It's not a joke. I mean it.'

'You're mad. I can't move to Melbourne, Seb. I've got work here. A life here.'

'What life? Back living at home, at Mum's beck and call? And you haven't got work, you've got penal servitude.'

'I'm fine.'

'You're not fine. I've been watching you since I got here. You've got that expression you used to have when you were little. This one.' He demonstrated it. A worried, anxious expression.

He had it exactly right. It was like looking in a mirror. She forced a smile. 'It's a nice idea –'

'A nice idea?'

'A really nice idea. But I can't just up and leave. Mum needs me here.'

'Sylvie, can I be blunt? Ever hear that story Cinderella? The one about the little servant girl and her cruel family? You're turning into her.'

'I'm not. I don't sit by the fire.' She pointed her toes. 'And I don't have glass slippers.'

'They treat you just as badly. Mum doesn't mean to, I know. She's self-centred, but she's not malicious. Heckle and Jeckle are different. I can imagine them today – fetch this, do that. Am I right?'

She knew her face gave her away. 'Today was an unusual day.'

'Why, because they noticed you? I've heard them talk to you like that whether it's a wedding or not. They're squashing you, Sylvie. They did it when you were little and they're doing it now. You need to get away from them. Why are you putting up with it?'

'I told you, I like being busy.'

'There's busy and there's being a mouse on a wheel. I'm worried about you.'

'Don't be.'

'Always have, always will. I'm serious about Melbourne, Sylvie. I'm also being selfish. I'm going away on a three-week shoot next month and I want a house-sitter. Someone to water my plants, keep my neighbours at bay. The person I'd lined up cancelled on me this week. I was about to advertise but now there's no need. You'd be perfect. And you'd be doing me a huge favour.'

'You're making that up.'

'I'm not making it up. I can show you the wording for the ad.'

'But I can't leave everyone here in the lurch.'

'What lurch? Vanessa's on honeymoon for the next month. Mum's going to her beach house to paint.' He refused to call it 'the retreat', as Fidelma did. 'Cleo's going on holiday as well, she told me. To Byron, I think. Or Palm Beach. Somewhere glamorous, anyway.'

'She is?' Cleo hadn't mentioned anything to Sylvie about a holiday. 'It'll be a good time to catch up while everyone's away, then,' she said, finding a bright voice. 'I've loads of filing to do. A new database to set up.'

'Can I ask you a direct question?'

'Your others weren't direct?'

He ignored her sarcasm. 'Are you happy, Sylvie? At work? At home? With life?'

'Deliriously.' To her dismay she felt a prickle of tears in her eyes. She blinked them away. 'It's the champagne. I'm fine. I'm absolutely fine.'

'It's not the champagne.' He drew her to the side of the dance floor and found her a chair. 'You used to say the same thing to me when you were little, you know, when Mum and Dad were screaming at each other. "I'm fine. Absolutely fine." You'd copied it from a British TV show. *Upstairs*, *Downstairs* or something.'

He was right, she had. She managed a smile. 'Well, I am fine. I'm absolutely fine.' She said it in a perfect cut-glass English accent.

He pulled up a chair beside her. 'I didn't believe you then and I don't now. What is it? What's happened?'

The combination of too much champagne, the exhaustion of the past few days and the concern on her brother's face prompted the truth. 'Something silly. I might have got it wrong, though. Misheard it.'

'Misheard what.'

'Mum.'

'Tell me.'

Sylvie knew she hadn't misheard it. Her mother had been pointing out her family to a guest at the wedding.

A dealer, Sylvie thought. Someone high up in the art world, at least. Fidelma had pointed out Cleo, and Vanessa, the beautiful bride. She'd said that Sebastian was on his way from Melbourne. 'You've heard of him, of course?' 'Of course,' the man had said. Fidelma had listed all their achievements, talked about the joys of an artistic household, of their dramatic sensibility as a family. Sylvie had heard most of it many times in interviews. 'And your other daughter?' the man had asked. 'You've three, haven't you?'

Sylvie hesitated before finishing. 'And Mum said to him, "Oh, yes, there's Sylvie, my youngest. But she doesn't really do anything."'

'I'll kill her,' Sebastian said.

'It's true, Seb. I don't do anything. Nothing lasting.'

'You work harder than anyone I know. You've got a degree. You haven't been out of work since you left uni. The only difference is you're not a bloody show pony about it.'

Sylvie was surprised at how angry he seemed. 'She's got a point. So do you. I am Cinderella. Look at our family, Seb. Artist, fashion designer, jeweller, lighting genius, secretary. Can you pick the odd one out?'

'You're not just a secretary and you know it. What was the name of that high-flying temp agency you used to work for? The one that sounded like a brothel?'

'Executive Stress Relief.' It was an agency specialising in emergency high-level secretarial support, for everyone from top business people to government ministers. Sylvie had been their employee of the year for the past four years. Her boss, Jill, had told her there was a position waiting back with them whenever she wanted.

'You've got them as a safety net, haven't you? If you were to leave Union Street?'

'Yes, but I'm not looking for a safety net.'

'No, what you need is an escape chute.' He was thoughtful for a moment. 'You remember when you were little, and I used to do those treasure hunts for you? With the dares?'

'Of course. You made me eat a worm once, do you remember?'

'I didn't make you. You mis-read the clue.'

Sylvie had loved those treasure hunts, Sebastian's birthday presents to her from the time she was eight until she turned fourteen. He'd devised a series of clues based on her favourite books. They'd taken her days to solve sometimes. Each one had led to a challenge or special treat of some sort. One year, she found herself up on the roof of the house, building a cubby from a bed sheet and a fold-up chair. Another year, he dared her to spend the night in the garden of their suburb's allegedly haunted house. She lasted all night, to Sebastian's amazement.

'I hereby resurrect the days of the treasure hunts. Sylvie Devereaux, I dare you to come to Melbourne.'

Sylvie laughed. 'Good one. You forgot the clues, though. And I'm not a kid any more.'

'Don't change the subject. Come on. I dare you. Even for a few weeks. Let's call it a trial run. A holiday. An escape.'

'Let's call it madness. I've got a job here.'

'That's all that's stopping you?'

'Yes, but –'

'Stay here.'

She watched as he went to their mother, then Vanessa, then Cleo. All three listened, nodded. They were soon smiling, laughing even. They adored Sebastian. Everyone did. He was back within five minutes. 'It's settled. You're coming to Melbourne.'

'Really? Just like that? And what did Mum say?'

'Do you want the truth?'

Sylvie nodded.

'She didn't bat an eyelid. I said, "Sylvie's worried about leaving work behind," and she said, "Oh, we'll get someone else from an agency. There's not much to it."'

The words felt like a punch. 'What about being in the house on her own?'

'Ray was doing the Revolting Tickling Thing on the back of her neck while she was talking.' Sebastian had

22

dubbed it that the last time he was home. 'So it looks like you're off the hook there as well.'

'And Vanessa and Cleo?'

'Thought it was a great idea. Just what you needed, they said.'

It was like being patronised, hit and encouraged, all at once. She'd half hoped her sisters would listen with alarm to Sebastian's suggestion, come across and say, 'But, Sylvie, what will we do without you?' She looked over. They were involved in animated conversations with their friends, as if Sebastian's suggestion had had no impact. She'd worked long days, nights and weekends for them. She thought she'd been making a difference, helping them, keeping the studio running.

She turned in time to see her mother move gracefully to the open window and stand within its frame, the curves of the Opera House a striking backdrop to her floaty dress and tumble of hair. The setting was no accident, Sylvie knew. Fidelma had a knack of posing for maximum visual impact. Ray joined her and began the Revolting Tickling Thing again. Sebastian was right, their on-again off-again relationship was clearly back on. Which meant Ray would soon be back living in the house, taking over the kitchen, prefacing all his sentences with, 'Fidelma's asked me to ask you . . .'

Two tables away, Great-Aunt Mill was talking loudly. 'I still don't know why everyone laughed,' she was saying. 'I was quite serious about her being my companion. I think we'd be very happy together.'

Sebastian was watching Sylvie's face closely. 'Well?'

She stood up. 'Ready when you are,' she said.

Chapter Three

For the third time since Sebastian had left for his film shoot that morning, Sylvie took herself on a tour of his Melbourne apartment.

It was on the second floor of a converted red-brick mansion in South Yarra, two streets from the Botanic Gardens. He'd moved in eight months before, after years of flat-shares with other theatre people around Melbourne. The apartment was like a stage set itself, with high ceilings, bay windows, polished wooden floorboards and ornate ceiling roses.

'If anyone wanted to do *This Is Your Life* on me, it's all here,' he'd said as he showed Sylvie around. The sofa was from an Oscar Wilde play he'd worked on. The chandelier from a modern Shakespeare. Paintings from an opera set. A mirror from a music video. The walls in the entrance hall were covered in framed photos of his friends and family. There was a futon in one bedroom, an elaborate carved sleigh-type bed in the other, rich red rugs on the floor of both. The whole effect was a cross between a flea market, an antiques store and backstage at a theatre. She loved it.

She hadn't moved down immediately after the wedding. Sebastian had asked for a week to get himself packed and organised for the film shoot. She'd used the time in Sydney to organise the already organised office at Union Street and leave notes for any incoming temp. She'd tidied up her already tidy bedroom in the family home. She met friends for farewell drinks and dinner. She had lunch with Jill, the boss of Executive Stress Relief, who made a point of taking all her Melbourne contact details. She was hoping to be there in the next few weeks and wanted to meet up again.

'I can actually picture you living in Melbourne,' she'd said to Sylvie. 'Are you planning on staying long?'

'A few weeks initially. With an eye to the long term.' It felt brave saying that. 'I'll get in touch with temp agencies and real estate agents as soon as I get there.'

Jill was impressed. 'You're certainly hitting the ground running.'

'That's the plan,' Sylvie said, hoping Jill couldn't see her fingers were crossed under the table.

Vanessa, Cleo and her mother had all left Sydney the day after the wedding. Vanessa left a message on the machine wishing Sylvie a safe trip and asking her to make sure the trade-fair orders had been dispatched. Cleo left a note saying have fun and asking her to collect her dry-cleaning before she went. Her mother took her out for a farewell coffee and talked the entire time about how wonderful it was to have Ray back in her life.

The only person in Sylvie's family who'd seemed interested in her trip to Melbourne was Great-Aunt Mill. She'd left messages on the office answering machine all week, either before Sylvie got in or late at night.

'I hear you're popping down to Melbourne for a little holiday with Sebastian, Sylvie. What a lovely idea. We'll be busy when you get back – Vincent left boxes and boxes of material to sort through – so I'm glad you'll be fresh.'

'Sylvie, I've found a gardener, so that's the outside of the house taken care of, while you and I make a start on the inside. Vincent wasn't much of a gardener, I'm afraid. Though he did like trees.'

'I was going to organise the painters for your room but you might like to choose the colours yourself, Sylvie. It's blue at the moment. Such a lovely aspect from that room. A view right over the city. There's a fig tree too. I've made delicious jam from it over the years. Vincent's favourite.'

'You're off tomorrow, I believe? Safe trip. Will you be

warm enough there? Vincent always hated Melbourne. Far too cold for him. I've got Sebastian's number so I'll be in touch if I need to.'

She'd ended each call with the same message. 'No need to ring back.'

'You *do* need to ring her back. You have to be straight with her,' Sebastian said after she told him about the calls. 'Just ring her and say, "Thanks again for the kind offer, but I'm not moving in with you, you crazy old coot."'

'She's not a crazy old coot.'

'She's the queen of crazy old coots.'

'She's just lonely. She must be missing Vincent a lot. And I don't want to hurt her feelings.'

Sylvie had always felt a bit sorry for Mill. She often seemed to be either lost in the crowd or ignored at family occasions, even though she was always the first to respond to any invitation. Fidelma was quite vague about who she actually was. Her late grandmother's sister, she finally remembered. Or was it cousin? They all called her Great-Aunt for convenience. Until she'd inherited Vincent's Surry Hills home, she'd lived in a small flat in Newtown, travelling across town for nearly forty years to work as his cook and cleaner, six days a week. She always arrived at family gatherings with several large plastic containers filled with her home-made biscuits, buns and exquisitely iced cakes.

Sylvie called her back and left a polite message on her

machine. 'Thanks for your calls, Mill. I'm not sure how long I'll be in Melbourne but I'll be in touch as soon as I know a bit more about my future plans.'

What future plans, she wondered as she walked through Sebastian's apartment again, a nervous feeling in her stomach. All her pre-trip bravado seemed to have evaporated, now she was here. It wasn't that she was worried about being in Melbourne on her own. She knew it reasonably well, having been down with Fidelma for several exhibition openings over the years. She was scared of something else. The reality of it not meeting the fantasy she'd built in her head all her life.

Melbourne had been her Utopia. Whenever things were difficult at home with her mother or sisters after the divorce, as a child and later as a teenager, she'd imagined herself living in Melbourne with Sebastian and her father. Sebastian had sent her postcards from there nearly every week in the early years. They had taken up almost a wall of her bedroom. She built whole stories around the photographs. That green tram was the one she and Sebastian would catch to school. The long street – Swanston Street – was where they would go walking on Sundays, Sebastian on one side of her, her father on the other. She imagined boat trips together on the Yarra in winter, picnics on the beach at St Kilda in summer. They'd go to see plays at the Arts Centre.

Football matches at the MCG. She would barrack for Essendon, she decided. She was the only girl in her class at school who knew all the Australian Rules football teams. She kept it to herself, though. She'd never told anyone about her secret Melbourne life. Not even Sebastian.

He had given her a soft and welcoming landing on this trip. He'd met her at Tullamarine airport, holding up a sign, wearing a peaked cap and guiding her outside to where a limousine was waiting. 'It's not every day Cinderella comes to stay,' he said. He admitted later that the owner of the car was a friend of his and had loaned it as a favour.

They had two days together before he left. He took her on a guided tour of the Botanic Gardens and treated her to coffee and cake in the café inside the gates. The trees were wearing the slightest tinge of autumn red and gold. They visited the nearby streets and shops in South Yarra, Richmond and Prahran. She met friends of his in the local milk bar, laundry, Greek restaurant, Thai restaurant and Japanese noodle bar.

He made a special point of taking her to a small bookshop three streets from his house. The owner, a smiling, grey-haired Scottish man in his early forties, looked up with pleasure as they came in.

'Here she is, Don,' Sebastian said, putting his arm around Sylvie. 'Sylvie, Donald. Donald, my little sister

Sylvie. She's my representative on earth while I'm away so please treat her with the respect and adoration you would normally show me.'

'Welcome, Sylvie,' Donald said, getting into the spirit, kissing her hand gallantly. 'Come and see us any time. Any sister of Sebastian's is, let me think, what's that saying –' he paused, 'hopefully less trouble than he is.'

'You'll miss me while I'm gone,' Sebastian said. He glanced around the shop. 'Is Max here?'

'Day off, Seb, sorry. I'll tell him you dropped in.'

As Donald turned to serve a customer, Sebastian spoke quietly to Sylvie. 'I really want you to meet Max. He's a very good friend of mine. I've asked him to keep an eye on you as well.'

Something in Sebastian's tone caught Sylvie's attention. A very good friend? As in more than a friend? As in the someone Sebastian had met recently? Her brother had always been good at getting personal details out of her, and keeping his own life secret. She had a hunch he'd just given away more than he realised.

'It'll be great to meet him,' she said.

At a farewell dinner the evening before, Sebastian had taken her to a small Italian restaurant a few blocks from his apartment. The handwritten menu had run to ten pages. When she'd asked him to order for her, he was appalled. 'You don't know about Italian food?'

'Of course I do. But you're the expert.'

'Then you have to become one, too. Italian food's one of the great pleasures of life, Sylvie.'

'I thought you told me dancing was.'

'Food – any kind of food, not only Italian – dancing, love and sleep. That's all anyone needs to be happy.'

Sylvie did like food and liked cooking too. She'd just got out of practice, living at home. As she explained to Sebastian, Fidelma had developed food allergies recently.

He raised an eyebrow. 'That would be from the same family of allergies that stopped you having real pets when you were little?'

Sylvie had forgotten what a good memory Sebastian had. As a seven-year-old, she'd invented an imaginary kitten, one that wouldn't give her mother allergies. She called it Silky, after the fairy in her favourite Enid Blyton books. Silky miraculously had kittens herself a few weeks later. Sylvie named them after her other favourite book characters. At one stage there were fifteen imaginary kittens living in her bedroom.

'Why do you hate Mum so much, Seb?' she asked now.

'I don't hate her. I actually enjoy her hugely. What I hate is how she controls you.'

'She doesn't.'

'No, of course she doesn't. And if she did, she doesn't any more because I have whisked you from under her sweet little allergic nose. So tell me, what were the last three meals you cooked?'

'For Mum and me?'

'For anyone.'

Sylvie thought back. 'Pasta with tomato sauce. Vegetable soup. Tofu and steamed vegetables.' Fidelma had been in a vegetarian phase. Six months earlier she had eaten nothing but steamed fish. Before that, only grilled organic meat.

'Not a spice or herb to be found? You are what you eat, Sylvie. No wonder your life has been so dull lately.'

'I told you, Mum's got a particular palate.'

'Sylvie, one more day there and you'd have turned into a blancmange yourself. I am going to dripfeed chilli and fish sauce into you while you sleep. We can work on you internally and externally. Spice up your life in more ways than one. We can rebuild you. We have the technology.' Sebastian held up his glass. 'To your trial run, Sylvie.'

'To my trial run.'

They clinked glasses.

An hour later, their main courses of homemade tortellini and potato gnocchi finished, she refilled their glasses and lifted hers in another toast. 'Thank you, Sebastian.'

'For what?'

'The wine. The dinner. The escape chute. The house-sitting. Everything.'

'Don't thank me yet. I'm hardly started.'

'What do you mean?'

'Mind your own business.' He called over the waiter then. 'Tiramisu to share, Sylvie? No, we're too old to share. Two servings of tiramisu, Tony, please.'

They ate their dessert, the rich coffee-soaked cake wrapped in thick cream. Their espresso coffees had just arrived when Sebastian shifted in his seat and said in a conversational tone, 'Did I tell you Dad's living in Collingwood these days?'

She had been waiting for Sebastian to mention him. It had been the one subject hanging between them since she arrived. She'd expected Fidelma to say something before she left too and been surprised when she hadn't. Perhaps she felt she didn't need to. Sylvie had heard it all so many times in her life she didn't need refreshing. 'He's a bad man, Sylvie. A lying, manipulative, cruel man.' 'Why would you want to go and visit him? I couldn't bear it if you did, Sylvie. It's enough for me to cope with that he took Sebastian from me.' 'Of course it's no surprise he hasn't sent you a birthday card, Sylvie. When did he ever think of anyone but himself?' Sylvie blinked, dismissing her mother's voice.

'Does he?' she said.

'Not that far from here. I can leave you his phone number if you want it.'

'Seb, I know what you're trying to do. It's too late.'

'Why? He's only in his sixties. He can still walk and talk.'

Sylvie knew that. She'd seen the occasional reference to him in the literary pages of the newspapers, whenever his poems were included in new anthologies. Even so many years on, Fidelma would rage against him if she saw his name or photograph. 'Look at him. Like butter wouldn't melt in his mouth.'

'Does he know I'm here?' Sylvie asked.

'I told him you were coming down, yes.'

'Then he can get in touch with me if he wants to, can't he?'

'I think he's too nervous.'

'Nervous?'

'He doesn't know what sort of reception he'd get.'

'Reception? I'm his daughter, not a werewolf.'

'So go and see him.'

She didn't answer for a moment. 'What's he like these days?'

'He drives a current Mercedes-Benz. He lives in a penthouse. He collects butterflies. He holds a black belt in karate. He speaks fluent Swahili.' Sebastian smiled. 'Or perhaps he does none of those things. Find out for yourself.'

'Do you see him often?'

'Once a month or so. We usually meet for dinner. He's got a favourite Malaysian place in Prahran. Or we talk on the phone or by email.'

'So you're close?'

'We agree on some things, disagree on others. I know what's happening in his life, to a degree. He knows a bit about me.'

'Do you like him?'

'Sylvie, Dad is a human being. Not a cartoon villain or however Mum has painted him. He's likable sometimes, other times he drives me crazy. He's complicated. Welcome to the world of parents. Do you like Mum?'

The million dollar question. Did she? She admired her, enjoyed her company much of the time, found her frustrating, stimulating. 'I love her. She's my mother.'

'You ignored the question. Skilfully, though, I'll give you that. You're off the hook for now.'

He called for the bill. On the way home to his apartment they called into a bar for a nightcap. He made her laugh with stories about badly behaved actors he'd worked with. They didn't speak about her father, or her mother, again.

Sylvie walked out into the hallway of Sebastian's apartment now and looked at the framed photographs once more.

One photo to the side caught her eye. It was an old

black and white of Mill, pictured sweeping the front verandah of her Newtown flat with a straw broom, squinting into the lens, her hair falling out of its bun as usual. Sebastian had stuck a Post-it note to the bottom of it: *Great-Aunt Mill prepares for her companion Sylvie's arrival.* He had stuck another note underneath a photo of Vanessa and Cleo arriving at an opening night in a limousine. *Heckle and Jeckle alight from their pumpkin and greet the masses.*

She recognised lots of the photos. Sebastian was famous for raiding cupboards and photo albums on visits home and taking whatever he wanted. He said it was because he was the product of a broken home, that he was psychologically disturbed and in constant need of reassurance and familiar objects around him.

He amazed her, how matter-of-fact, even jokey, he was about it. She remembered the time of the divorce with only a tight feeling in her chest. She'd known of course that her parents weren't happy together. There'd been no way of not knowing. Creative people like her parents had found creative ways to abuse and insult one another.

There were several photos of the two of them, though none together. The ones of her father looked recent. She looked at them closely. She hadn't seen him in the flesh since she was eight years old.

Her idea of him had constantly changed since that

time, influenced by whatever she was reading or watching. As a child, she'd thought of him as an Uncle Quentin-type distracted scientist character from the *Famous Five* books. The missing Mr March from *Little Women*. The absent father in *The Railway Children*.

The real Laurence Devereaux had an oval-shaped face, grey curly hair and enquiring eyes. Sebastian was very like him. Sylvie had often been told how like Sebastian she was.

Which meant she was like her father too.

CHAPTER FOUR

By the end of the first week of her trial run, Sylvie had learned one new thing about herself.

She was no good at relaxing.

She'd walked into the city centre every day, via the Botanic Gardens, taking a different path each time to get to know her way around. She'd contacted five real estate agents to get an idea about current rents in nearby suburbs. She'd rung three temp agencies, faxed her CV and Sydney references to them all, done face-to-face interviews with two, phone interviews with the other one and was now on call for work with all three.

She'd asked herself a hundred questions and had a head full of possible answers. If I stayed here permanently, which suburb would I live in? What work would I do? Would I make any friends? Where would I eat out? Where would I stop for coffee after work?

Where would I have long Sunday breakfasts? Where would I shop? Go dancing? See films? Underneath all of them was one big question. Would I be the same person I am in Sydney?

Sebastian rang to see how she was getting on. He was on location in an old country mansion halfway between Melbourne and Adelaide, working on a period drama. He was appalled when she told him what she'd been doing.

'What happened to the holiday? You're there to take some time out too, remember, not launch yourself on a full-scale reconnaissance mission.'

'It's a trial run. I'm trial running.'

'You're like an athlete on steroids. Slow down, would you? You have to have a gap in your life if you want something new to come in. Have you read a book? Watched a film? Listened to some calming music?'

'I haven't had time.'

He laughed. 'Then make time. And will you promise me something?'

'Depends.'

'Be home tomorrow between noon and one.'

'Why?'

'Just promise.'

She did as she was told. She got up early the next day, went to the shops down the road and bought all the ingredients for a leisurely holiday-type breakfast: fresh orange juice, warm croissants, ripe peaches and two newspapers.

She read them from front to back. She took out the folder Sebastian had left for her, labelled *Possible Leisure Activities and Cultural Pursuits for Sylvie in My Absence*. There were theatre programs, cinema schedules, opening times for the nearby swimming pool, library, gym and video store, all with Post-it notes and comments attached. She made a list of things she'd like to see.

Tucked underneath them all, she found an old-fashioned luggage label. 'Pin this to your clothes every time you go out', he'd written on another Post-it note. The label read: *My name is Sylvie. I live on Marne Street, South Yarra. I am lost. Please look after me.* She grinned as she attached it to her red denim jacket, feeling like Paddington Bear.

By eleven o'clock she was fidgety. At work by this time, she would have made twenty phone calls, sent thirty emails, filled a dozen orders and probably booked her mother or sisters into either a restaurant, a beautician or their latest fad, Club Dance, a mid-morning exercise class in a nearby nightclub. Sylvie had read the brochure as she booked her sisters in for a six-week course. For a small fortune, they were being promised new levels of fat-burning and mood-lifting. When Sylvie wondered out loud if this was a clever way of using the club during daylight hours, she'd been subjected to eye-rolling and accusations of being *so* pedestrian.

Maybe there was something to it. She was on her own,

in Melbourne, it was light outside and she was sober, but too bad. She found a *Best of the 80s* CD in Sebastian's large collection. From what she'd seen, all her neighbours left for work early, so she hoped for no complaints. She pushed back the furniture in the living room, turned the music up loud and danced to Dexy's Midnight Runners' 'Geno' and Spandau Ballet's 'Gold'. Midway through a Duran Duran song, the polished floorboards gave her an idea. She took off her sneakers and started sliding from room to room in her sock-covered feet. She changed CDs, finding Ravel's 'Bolero' and turning that up full blast as well. She did both Torvill and Dean's actions, making herself laugh. She and Sebastian had loved floor-skating as children, until Fidelma laid carpet in the hallway and main rooms. The dust coming up through the floorboards made her sneeze, she'd said.

Sylvie hadn't heard from her mother since leaving Sydney. She'd almost rung her four times. Each time she'd stopped. Fidelma was probably still at her coastal retreat. With Ray. Painting. Meeting her dealer. There was the shimmer of hurt that her mother hadn't rung to see how she was getting on, but it was a feeling she'd become used to over the years. It wasn't malice on Fidelma's part, as Sebastian had pointed out. It was absentmindedness. It still hurt.

As she slid to a halt near the answering machine in the hall, the light was flashing. Two messages. She hadn't heard the phone ring over the music. She pressed the button.

'Great-Aunt Mill calling, Sylvie. I've had a marvellous idea. Would you please start keeping a note of some handy household hints for me? All tried and tested. I'm getting forgetful so I think the best thing is to tell you when I think of them. Carla next door says I should buy one of those Dictaphone gadgets but I thought, no, that's silly. I can tell you and you're young and you'll remember for me. Denture-cleaning tablets are ideal for bleaching white table linen. So simple, isn't it? Thank you, Sylvie. No need to call back.'

The second message was from her sister Cleo. Her voice filled the hallway.

'Hi, Seb. Hi, Sylvie. Hope Melbourne's good. Sylvie, I can't find that dry-cleaning anywhere. We're back in Sydney for an opening night and I need my blue dress. Where did you put it?'

Sylvie hadn't put it anywhere. In the flurry of packing and getting ready to leave, she'd forgotten to get it. Oh bloody hell. She could call a courier and ask them to collect it and drop it around to Cleo. They should be able to give it to her without the docket. She'd ring them first and –

She stopped. Or she could ring Cleo back and tell her she was sorry, she'd forgotten, but perhaps Cleo could collect her own dry-cleaning.

She dialled the number before she lost her nerve. She could almost hear her heart beating. Voicemail, please, voicemail. Her plea was answered. 'Cleo, it's Sylvie.' Her voice was croaky. She gave a little cough. 'Hi, all's great here. Sebastian's apartment is beautiful. The weather's good. Um, your dry-cleaning –' About to back down and say she'd organise it from there, she had a vision of Sebastian frowning at her, mouthing, 'Don't let them bully you. Stand up for yourself.' She stood up straight. 'I'm sorry, but unfortunately I didn't get time to collect it. The docket's in the in-tray on the desk in the studio. Hope your holiday's going well. See you.'

She had to stop herself phoning back and apologising again. She went out for a walk around the block, away from the temptation. When she got back fifteen minutes later, there was another message.

She pressed the button. Cleo, again. 'Hi, Sylvie. Thanks for letting me know about the dry-cleaning. What a complete bloody pain in the backside. We're only in town for a few hours and I haven't got time to visit a dry-cleaners. I thought I could trust you to do that before you left.' A sigh. 'All right, look, don't worry about it, I'll do it myself. See you.'

Any mood-lifting the dancing had done was wiped out.

At exactly noon, the doorbell sounded. A tall, thin, red-haired woman about her own age was at the front door, dressed in a strappy top, skinny jeans and heels. Sylvie barely had time to say hello before the other woman started talking.

'Sylvie? Of course you're Sylvie, who else? I'm Leila, Seb's neighbour across the courtyard.' She glanced down and her lips twitched. 'I like the name tag. Has it come in handy?'

Sebastian's label was still pinned to Sylvie's jacket. She hurriedly unpinned it, realising she'd also been for a walk around the block wearing it. 'It's a joke, I promise. Seb's idea of a joke, at least.'

'What's got into him lately? I spent a day last week with a Post-it note saying "I'm a monkey, give me a banana" on my back. He thought it was hilarious.'

'I'm so sorry. We thought the electric shock treatment was working.'

Leila smiled again, a dimple appearing in her cheek. 'Time to up the voltage, I think.' She took an envelope out of her bag. 'He asked me to drop this in to you today.'

Sylvie glanced at it, front and back. No clues there. 'Thanks very much.'

'Seb says you're down for a few weeks or maybe longer, is that right? Fancy a drink or something some night?'

'I'd love that, thanks.' Leila reminded Sylvie of someone. Pippi Longstocking, she realised, one of her favourite childhood book characters. She warmed to her even more. 'Would you like a coffee or something now?'

'Normally, yes please. I live on coffee. But I'm running late for an audition.' She pulled a face. 'I'm up for a part in one of the soaps today, hence this charming outfit. Another time maybe?'

'That'd be great, drop in any time. And good luck with the audition.'

'I need it, believe me. See you!' With a cheery wave, she was down the stairs and away.

Leila's visit cancelled out the effect of Cleo's phone message. Envelope in hand, Sylvie turned on the music again and went for a final slide around the apartment. As Patrick Hernandez's 'Born To Be Alive' came to an end, she arrived in the kitchen, took out a knife and carefully slit open the envelope.

Inside was a sheet of fax paper. On it, four lines in Sebastian's handwriting. Not last-minute instructions about the house-sitting. Nor tips about good restaurants or cafés or job websites or house agencies.

Sylvie smiled. It was something even better.

By mid-afternoon, the kitchen table was littered with scraps of paper covered in scribbles. There was a pile of books on the floor. Sylvie was on the phone.

'I can't figure it out, Seb. You have to give me a clue.'

It had taken her an hour to get hold of him. It was a bad line. 'Sorry, no can do, Miss Devereaux,' he said, his voice breaking in and out. 'It's a treasure hunt not a treasure-handed-to-you-on-a-plate.'

'But I can't decipher the riddle. And I've been through every book on your bookshelf.' She'd opened every single one and there were no slips of paper to be found.

'That's cheating going straight to the books. You're supposed to look when you've deciphered the title, not flick through willy-nilly.'

'I was getting desperate. We can change the rules, can't we?'

'The rules are set in stone and shall be forevermore. Apart from the fact I had to fax this starter clue down to Leila, but these were extraordinary circumstances. Anyway, who said anything about my bookshelf?'

'Where else should I look for a book? In the fridge?'

'Oh, you wit. There are other places for books, you know.'

'Libraries, you mean? You want me to go the library?'

He lapsed into a Scottish accent. 'Och, pet, there are other places than libraries.'

Scottish. When had she heard a Scottish accent recently? Donald in the bookshop. 'The bookshop? Do you mean your friend's bookshop?'

'Is that the time? Got to go, Sylvie.' He hung up.

She pulled on her sneakers, picked up her bag and jacket and set off. The area already seemed familiar. Quiet roads lined with elegant stone houses beside modern apartments, all leading to the long shopping street. The sky was blue, but there was an autumn crispness to the air and a few brown leaves crunching underfoot.

As she walked, she thought back to the first of Sebastian's treasure hunts, a present for her eighth birthday. She remembered it so clearly, the one lovely thing in a time of turmoil. For the months beforehand, the mood in the family house had been an unhappy one. Her parents always seemed to be fighting. Odd things started happening. Sylvie's favourite painting of a small boat, an inheritance from Fidelma's grandmother, disappeared off the living room wall. So did the gold lamp in the hallway. Her father started staying out all night, coming home as Sylvie was on her way to school. He left one night with a suitcase. That time he didn't come back for a week. Her mother was either crying or angry all the time. She stayed in bed or sat on the back verandah. She rarely went into the studio. If she did, her paintings were angry splashes of colour, dark lines, fierce shapes.

Sylvie's birthday arrived. There was the present of a jigsaw puzzle, unwrapped, but no party and no cake. Her mother told her she was sorry, but she couldn't manage it. Vanessa and Cleo were otherwise occupied.

Already a tight duo, they spent most of their time in their shared bedroom talking makeup and fashion, or out with their friends. There was no point asking them to help her make a birthday cake. Sebastian returned home late that night from an interstate theatre camp. He noticed there were no party leftovers. She heard him go in to their mother, heard raised voices. 'She's only a little kid. Couldn't you have done *something* special for her?' She didn't hear her mother's reply.

The next day Sylvie woke to find an envelope with her name on it at the end of her bed. A sheet of paper was inside. She opened it. It was Sebastian's writing.

> A chair that grows wings?
> Lands of pixies and elves?
> If you want the next clue,
> Better look on the shelves!

It took her nearly an hour to figure it out. Sebastian wouldn't help. 'It's a treasure hunt, Sylvie. You have to work it out.' She eventually realised what it meant. A chair with wings. The wishing chair. It was the name of one of her favourite Enid Blyton books. She found it on her bookshelf. She looked at the front cover, on the back. No clues there. She flicked through the pages. There tucked in the middle was another slip of paper. On it, two sentences of jumbled words.

Og ot het ozo. Kool ta eth gritse.

It took her an hour to figure them out, too. 'Go to the zoo? Look at the tigers?' she asked Sebastian. 'Is that what it says?'

'If that's what it says, then we'd better do it. Come on.'

They caught the ferry across the harbour and then a bus to the top of the hill. At the zoo, in front of the tigers' enclosure, he gave her another slip of paper. It told her to go to the café. They had chips and an ice-cream, as directed. Another slip of paper. To the harbour for another ferry ride, to Manly this time. Another slip of paper. To a bookshop. There behind the counter was a parcel with her name on it. Five Enid Blyton books. It was the best birthday of her life.

Until they got home that night and heard the news. Their parents were getting divorced.

Things grew worse. She heard her mother talking to her friends in her studio, using words she didn't understand. Division of assets. Maintenance payments. Custody battles. As a child, she'd thought they were saying custardy. Fighting over custard? Why would they do that? Sebastian explained it to her. The family was going to be divided up.

The idea terrified her. 'I want to be with you, Sebbie. Wherever you are.'

'Sylvie, it won't be up to me.'

'Please, Seb. Please let me go with you.'

She was taken into an office, a room with a high ceiling and five red chairs. A woman behind a desk asked her in a kind voice where she would like to live. She didn't have to think twice. 'I want to be with my brother.'

'And if your brother was living with your father?'

'I want to be with my brother.'

In the end it didn't matter what she said. The judge decided. Sebastian was going to live with his father in Melbourne. Laurence Devereaux had been appointed to a position in the English department at Melbourne University. Fidelma was given custody of her three daughters, Vanessa, Cleo and Sylvie Devereaux. Case closed.

The day at the courtroom was the last time she'd seen her father. He'd come over to her and leaned down as if he was about to speak. Sylvie's mother took the top of her arm in a tight hold and pulled her away. There had been a bruise there the next day.

Sylvie reached Donald's bookshop, nestled between a French bakery and a wine shop. The front windows featured beautifully displayed books and posters. An old-fashioned bell sounded as she pushed open the glass door.

Without Sebastian sweeping her along beside him, she had more time to look around the shop. Pale wood shelves, a skylight, the walls painted calm colours, each section clearly marked: fiction, non-fiction, Australian, new releases, poetry, classics. Two tables at the front of the shop featured staff picks, recently reviewed titles and special promotion titles. To the side was a children's section divided not into fiction or non-fiction but into subjects: cats, dogs, trains, trucks. Classical music played softly. The whole shop smelt of coffee. Towards the back was a small café with three tables, armchairs and a compact coffee-making machine, the shelf above it lined with colourful cups and large glass jars filled with biscuits. There were half a dozen customers browsing the shelves and book tables.

The only assistant was up a ladder, putting up a poster. As she waited by the counter, he descended. She saw black runners. Long legs in faded jeans. A blue T-shirt. Lightly tanned arms. A head of dark-brown curls. It wasn't Donald.

The man turned as he reached the floor. He had a boyish sprinkling of freckles on his face. Dark eyes. A grown-up Huckleberry Finn, Sylvie thought. First Pippi Longstocking, now this man. She felt like she'd stumbled into Book Land at the top of the Faraway Tree.

He smiled at her. 'Hi. Sorry to keep you waiting. Can I help you?'

'Hello. Yes please. I was wondering if Dona—'

He interrupted. 'You're Sylvie, aren't you? Sebastian's sister?' At her nod he gave a big smile. 'He said you'd be calling in. You're exactly as he said you'd be.'

She wondered what Sebastian had said. Lost-looking? Anxious? She put on a bright expression, just in case. 'Which means you must be Max.'

He bowed. 'At your service. How did you know? Let me guess, he described me as a devastatingly good-looking man of the world?'

She smiled. 'Nearly. He said you were a very good friend of his.'

'And I am, for my sins.' He put out a hand. 'It's great to meet you. Are you looking for a book or a coffee? Both, maybe?'

'Actually, something a bit more complicated than that.'

'Excellent.' He leaned against the counter and folded his arms. 'I'm in the mood for something a bit more complicated today. Ask away.'

She reached into her bag for the envelope. 'When we were young, Sebastian and I used to –'

'You're on to the treasure hunt already?'

'You know about it?'

'I couldn't possibly say. But you don't waste any time, I'll give you that.'

She took out the piece of paper. 'He's left me the starter clue but I –'

Max put his hands over his ears and shut his eyes. 'Sorry, I can't help you.'

'You can't?'

He shook his head, eyes still shut. 'Seb said no

matter how much you begged, you had to figure it out for yourself.'

'But can you tell me if I'm in the right place? Will I find the book here?'

He opened one eye. 'We've got twenty thousand books here so the odds are good. Any questions about them, feel free to ask. Though perhaps not twenty thousand questions this afternoon. We close at seven.'

'Can you help me at all?'

'I'm a highly trained bookshop assistant, with a mind like a computer, of course I can help you. But only with book-specific questions.'

She liked the spark of mischief in his eyes. If he was Sebastian's new partner, then she approved completely. 'Did you have a hand in this?'

Another grin. 'Let me just say that when Sebastian burns the midnight oil or gets a notion about doing something, he doesn't like doing it on his own. And that's the last bit of information you're getting. How about a coffee before you get started?'

'Could you make it a strong one?'

Ten minutes later, settled at a table at the back of the shop, a double espresso in front of her, she went over Sebastian's clue again. She'd read it so many times she knew it off by heart.

In search of a new and glittering vocation?
Then, dear Sylvie, travel old-fashioned kilometres
Across an ancient story-filled river.

His message was clear. He was telling her she needed to leave Sydney – the 'fashion' referred to Vanessa, the 'glittering' to Cleo's jewellery, she'd guessed – to find what she was supposed to be doing with her life. But what river had she crossed – or flown over at least – to get from Sydney to Melbourne? The Murray? Was she supposed to look in books about the Murray River?

Max was serving an elderly man. She waited a little back from the counter watching him. He had a lovely manner with the customer, friendly but respectful. He looked over and smiled at her as the man left.

'You've solved the puzzle already?'

'Inching closer every minute. I think I'm onto something. Would you have any books set on or about the Murray River?'

'Fiction or non-fiction? Or friction or non-friction, as my grandmother used to say.'

She smiled. 'Either. All. Any.'

He was very helpful. He checked on the computer, flicked through catalogues, searched the shelves with her. They found two fiction titles quickly. *The River Kings* by Max Fatchen. *All the Rivers Run* by Nancy Cato. There were also five works of non-fiction. She flicked through the pages of each of them. Nothing.

'It wouldn't have fallen out, would it?' she asked. 'It's usually only a little slip of paper.'

'I have no idea what you're talking about.'

'How long would it take me to check every book on every shelf here, do you think?'

'I've just done a part-time, manual stocktake so I can tell you – three weeks, two days and one long, heart-breaking final hour. Isn't that cheating, though? And have you got that long?'

'Would you mind me working through the night?'

'Of course not. You can sleep in the poetry section if you need to.'

'Is that a clue? It's in the poetry section?'

'No, I was trying to be funny. The poetry section being the quietest place.' He gave a rueful smile. 'Not that funny, obviously. I need new material.'

'No, it was. It was funny. I was laughing on the inside.'

He assumed a sad expression. 'If you're looking for me, I'll be in the comedy self-help section.'

She returned to the café, still smiling. She read the clue again. It was definitely more complicated than the ones they'd done as children. But the principle was the same, surely. Break it down, Sebastian used to say. Line by line. Make lists of all the possibilities.

She found a book on geography, listing dozens of terms for measuring distances. Furlongs. Roods. Perch. Miles.

Yards. She wrote them down. Australian rivers? Darling. Torrens. Swan. Fitzroy. Franklin. Yarra. Margaret. *Margaret*. The author's first name? She underlined it.

She consulted dictionaries, thesauruses, atlases and guidebooks. When he wasn't serving customers and unpacking boxes, Max kept her supplied with coffee. He refused any money. 'It's all on Sebastian's tab. Whatever you want. He insisted.'

She listed words for glittering and vocation. Shining. Bright. Brilliant. Clear. Glossy. Luminous. Silver. Radiant. Job. Occupation. Career. Vocation. Duty. Position. Trade. Work.

Nothing. Just a swirl of words in her brain. She decided to distract herself with a quick walk and some fresh air and hope her subconscious would take over. It often worked when she was doing cryptic crosswords.

Max was at the counter, serving a customer. She mouthed that she'd be back in a moment and got a nod and smile in reply.

She was barely six shops away, just beyond the Italian restaurant, when it came to her. *Glittering vocation. Old-fashioned kilometres. Ancient river.* She ran back to the bookshop and threw open the door.

'*My Brilliant Career* by Miles Franklin,' she shouted.

The man at the counter looked up in surprise. Not Max, but Donald. 'Sylvie, how nice to see you again.'

CHAPTER FIVE

'So if I decided on the spur of the moment to hold a conference for five hundred people in four different languages and needed a fleet of secretaries, I could call you and you'd organise and manage the whole thing for me? Take shorthand? Work the computers? Organise everything?'

'Blindfolded,' Sylvie said, laughing. 'Arms tied behind my back.'

'That might make typing tricky, but never mind. You're not a secretary, you're Supertemp. Mental note, Max. If in need of multilingual conference, call Sylvie immediately.'

They'd been in the bar together for the past hour. Five doors down from the bookshop, it was small and Spanish-themed, with tapas on offer, flamenco music playing quietly in the background, and brightly coloured walls and dim lamps creating an intimate atmosphere.

She noticed his empty glass. 'It's your turn to answer questions. As soon as I get you another glass of wine.'

'My life is an open book. Very dull.' He stood up. 'And I got off early from work because of you, so the drinks are on me. Same again?'

She nodded. It had been Donald's idea for the two of them to go for a drink. He'd been very amused after she'd launched herself through the door of his shop, startling not only him but also his customers. Max had emerged laughing from behind the non-fiction shelves.

Donald waved away her apologies. 'It's nice to see someone so enthusiastic about their reading matter. Let me see, if my highly tuned intuition as a bookseller is right, you're quite interested in taking a look at *My Brilliant Career* by Miles Franklin? Now, where would that be, I wonder? Max, have you seen it?'

'I think we sold the last copy,' Max said. 'Just after Sylvie went for her walk.'

'Never mind. We could put an order in. An Australian classic like that, let me think, I could have it in within the week?'

'You're tormenting me now,' Sylvie said. 'I'm calling Consumer Affairs.'

'Sebastian was right about her, wasn't he, Donald?' Max said. 'How was it he described her to us? "A bright-eyed cutie?"'

'That was it. But he certainly didn't mention her

habit of shouting book titles at the top of her voice. They obviously have different shopping habits in Sydney. Max, loyal assistant, could you please show this bright-eyed young lady to our classics section?'

The Fs were on the second row from the top. Max reached up easily and took down the only copy. 'Shall I wrap that for you, madam? Or will you be ripping straight into the pages here and now?'

'Right here and now, thank you.'

She found the slip of paper in seconds. It was in the centre pages, folded in three. Sebastian had kept up the tradition of their childhood treasure hunts. There was a whole page of writing, all in jumbled letters. She looked up. Max was smiling at her.

'Did you know it was here the whole time?' she asked.

He nodded. 'I put it there. Sebastian couldn't reach.'

'So I could have bribed you when I came in this morning?'

'It would have been quicker. But look at all the practice you gave me making coffee. And now I'm an expert on the Murray River. That kind of knowledge can't be bought.'

He returned from the bar now with two glasses of wine. 'Here you are,' he said. 'A fine fruity shiraz from the Yarra Valley. Or perhaps it's a spicy cabernet from the Clare Valley. Or a cheeky full-bodied merlot from the Hunter Valley. I can't remember. It's a glass of red wine, anyway.'

'My favourite kind. Thanks, Max.'

He settled into his seat opposite her again.

'So, the trip to Melbourne is –' he said.

'So do you like working in the –' she asked.

They both laughed. 'You first,' Max said.

'I was going to ask if you liked working in the bookshop. And if you're originally from Melbourne.'

'Excellent questions, thank you. If you had asked them, I would have said yes to both before skilfully turning the conversation on its head and asking you what it was like to grow up in the middle of an artistic family like yours.' He paused. 'And then I would realise from the expression on your face that you've been asked that question far too many times and that is, of course, one of the reasons you left Sydney, so I would hurriedly backtrack and ask you an innocuous question about the weather.'

'Sorry. It was that obvious?'

He nodded. 'You've got one of those faces that gives a lot away. You'd make a good actress.'

'If I could act, yes.'

'You never tried?'

She shook her head. 'I can't paint, make jewellery or design clothes either, in case you were going to ask.'

'I wasn't, but that's good to know. I can't either, as it happens.'

She rubbed at her cheek, embarrassed. 'Sorry, Max. That wasn't fair.'

'Dr Max Reynolds, Family Therapist, is now in session. Would you like an appointment?'

She wanted to talk to him about it, she realised. 'Have you got a few hours?'

'Days, if needed. And they've got loads of wine behind the bar. I checked.'

'I don't know how much Sebastian told you –'

'Nothing too incriminating, I promise. He said he thought you were drowning in a sea of family, so he threw you a lifeline.'

'That's it in a nutshell. Embarrassing, isn't it? Nearly thirty and still being looked after by my big brother.'

'Not so big. What is he, five foot seven? A titch. A titch brother. And don't be embarrassed about it. We need our families to drive us crazy. Otherwise no one would ever go anywhere and what would get done in the world?'

'You think that?'

'I know it.'

'It's the same for you?'

He nodded. 'I'm the oldest of three boys. Mum and Dad are both doctors, with their own practice. There were expectations, obligations really, that I would become a doctor too.' He'd enrolled for med school before he knew it, he told her. Graduated, worked in the practice, knowing the whole time something was wrong. 'Then about four years ago I joined an amateur theatre group and that's when I realised what I wanted. Stage sets and scripts, not stethoscopes or charts. The production side, not the acting. The next week I enrolled to do stage management at the college of the arts. I've worked in theatre ever since. It's more precarious than medicine, but I love it.'

'So the bookshop is a part-time job?'

He nodded. 'Three days a week. It keeps me going between plays. That's how I met Sebastian. We worked on a production together last year. In fact, he got me the job in the bookshop. He's very good at looking after people.'

'And how did changing direction go down with your family? Your parents?'

'They loved it. Thought it was a fantastic idea.' He gave a quick smile. 'They were furious. I was ignored for a few months. Shouted at for another month. Four generations of the family in medicine. Who did I think I was, breaking with tradition? I needn't think they'd support me, etcetera etcetera.'

'Your brothers weren't interested either?'

'Not four years ago. It's changed now. My youngest brother's applied to do medicine, so my parents are mollified for the moment.' He gave a shrug. 'There it is. I can't condemn them for it. They're traditional. Old-fashioned. They also care too much what other people think about them. Social standing, that kind of thing.'

She'd had too much wine to be diplomatic. 'But they're okay about you and Sebastian?'

'Sorry?'

'About the two of you?'

'The two of us?'

'Being a couple.'

'Sebastian and I being a couple?' At her nod, he threw back his head and laughed. 'You thought Sebastian and I were together?'

'Aren't you?'

'Where did you get that idea?'

'He said that you were a very good friend of his and he had a kind of glint in his eye.'

'A glint?' He grinned. 'Sylvie, I'm sorry. Much as I'd love to be your brother-in-law, Sebastian and I bat for different teams. And as far as I can tell, Sebastian and Donald are very happy together without me interfering.'

'Donald?'

'Donald and Sebastian are together. You didn't know?'

'He said he was seeing someone. I got it into my head that it was you . . .'

Max laughed again. 'That's it. Tomorrow I start growing a beard. Taking bodybuilding classes. Injecting testosterone.'

'I didn't . . . I hope you don't . . . You didn't seem . . .' She stopped trying. 'Sorry.'

'It's fine. It means I'm in touch with my sensitive side. That's a good thing, surely.'

'A very good thing.'

'No harm done, then. Come on, let's get out of here.'

'Where are we going?'

'To a lap-dancing club. I've got a few things to prove.' He grinned at her expression. 'No, not a lap-dancing club. I'm taking you to dinner. I've got a lot of ground to make up.'

As they walked two blocks away to a small Greek restaurant, the mood changed between them. Over dinner, there was more conversation, occasional quick touches on each other's sleeves or hands. Either Max felt he had something to prove, or they had naturally tipped from conversation into a kind of flirting. Sylvie wasn't sure. All she knew was it had changed from being a night out with her brother's partner to feeling something more like a date. It was a very good feeling.

He walked her home afterwards. The restaurant was only ten minutes from Sebastian's apartment. The houses were mostly dark, a few cars driving down the side streets, a chill in the air. They stopped at the front of the apartment building. There were lights on behind curtains, the faint sound of a cello drifting down through an open window.

Max looked up at Sebastian's apartment and sighed. 'Ah, my love nest. My heart pounds to think of the nights I've spent there.'

'I'm sorry, I promise you. Which of us will ring Seb first and tell him, do you think?'

'I'll leave that to you. Give him my love, won't you?' He laughed. 'I mean it. I do love Sebastian.'

'I'm sure he loves you too.'

'I really enjoyed tonight, Sylvie. Drop in to the shop any time. Or give me a ring at home if you feel like a coffee.' He scribbled a number on the back of a receipt. 'I work odd hours so I'll be free when you least expect it.'

'And me too. I mean, ring here if you want to as well. Thanks, Max. For the wine and dinner and everything.'

'You're very welcome.' He touched the side of her face, a quick, sweet gesture. 'It's nice to have you here.'

'It's nice to be here.' A moment where they smiled at each other. A moment when she wanted to say, what about a drink tomorrow night? Or dinner at the end of the week? She left it too long. 'Goodnight.'

She turned as she reached the top of her stairs. He was still there. He raised a hand in a wave.

She rang Sebastian as soon as she got inside. He laughed at the case of mistaken identity. He was very glad she'd found the clue. He was also glad at the news of her drink and dinner with Max.

'Are you matchmaking, Seb?'

'Not actively,' he said. 'Just letting chemistry do its work. I like Max, I like you, therefore I assumed if I put Max with you, you would like each other. And being the magician I am, it happened. Prince Charming rides into your life.'

'But I'm not looking for Prince Charming.'

'Of course you're not. You've got far more serious problems than your love life.'

'Thanks very much.'

'I just thought it might be nice for you to meet someone who isn't a stinking deceitful social-climbing two-timing bastard like David. That's how you summed him up, wasn't it?'

'I think you left out two-faced.'

She still felt stupid thinking about David. It had taken her five months with him before she realised it was her Devereaux surname he was interested in, not her. She'd met him at one of her mother's exhibition openings. A lawyer studying art history in his spare time, he'd been full of opinions and talk of reviving the artistic salon tradition. He'd swept Sylvie off her feet. Her mother and sisters had been hugely flattered by his attention too. They'd come to the parties he'd thrown, cheerfully posed for the society photographers who often seemed to turn up. It took Sylvie far too long to realise what was going on. The clincher was when he began introducing her not as 'my girlfriend Sylvie', but as 'my dear friend Sylvie, one of the Devereaux family of artists'.

She'd brought it up on the way back to his apartment in Double Bay one night. 'I don't know why you keep saying that, David. I'm not an artist.'

'I can hardly introduce you as just a secretary, can I?'

She finished it with him that night. He pursued her with flowers and apologies until she gave him a second chance. He threw another party to celebrate. He invited her family again and spent most of the night talking to Fidelma. It ended when Sylvie saw a photo of him in the Sunday gossip pages, photographed beside the daughter of a well-known Sydney actor. He'd told Sylvie he was working back late that night. That time he accepted it was over. The next day he sent flowers to Fidelma, Vanessa and Cleo, saying it had been a pleasure to meet each of them. He sent them to the office. Sylvie was the only one there. She'd had to sign for them.

'And you liked Donald?' Sebastian said now.

She could hear the vulnerable tone in his voice. 'I liked him very much.'

'Good.' He was smiling now. She could hear that too.

'That's very good. Now get to bed. You've a lot of un-puzzling to do in the morning.'

It wasn't until after she'd cleaned her teeth and was about to get into bed that she checked the answering machine. It was flashing. One message. Max, she thought. Leaving a message already. She pressed the button.

'Sylvie, Mill here. Two quick thoughts. White vinegar makes a marvellous fabric softener. Just add a quick splash to the final rinse. And cider vinegar added to chooks' drinking water stops them getting worms. All for now. Goodnight. No need to call back.'

CHAPTER SIX

It took Sylvie one pot of coffee, two chocolate croissants and one and a half hours the next morning to un-jumble the dares. By Sebastian's standards, they were mild. No leaping off tall buildings. No eating of worms or spiders or caterpillars.

He'd set her three dares. She could spread them out over the next week or get the whole lot over and done with in a day. It was up to her. He wanted full reports, preferably typed or in Powerpoint form, but he would also settle for quick calls or messages left on his mobile phone. He would prefer it if she did them in the order listed but he gave her permission to be flexible.

The list was titled *Sylvie's Three-Step Search for Certainty*.

One: Ask someone out on a date.

Two: Host a dinner party. Dishes must contain the following ingredients: coriander, fish sauce, sesame oil, chilli, rice wine, galangal, lemongrass and Kaffir lime leaves.

Three: To be divulged when dares one and two are successfully completed.

The phone rang before she had a chance to start thinking about them. She snatched it up before it went to the answering machine. It was Mill.

'Oh, what a shame to get you, Sylvie,' she said immediately. 'I've really started to prefer answering machines. So much more efficient. No need to ask how are you, what have you been doing, how's the weather etcetera, don't you find? You can get straight to the point.'

'I can hang up if you like.'

Mill gave a roar of laughter. 'That would teach me. I must say I do like that cheeky little spirit of yours. I was just talking about you, in fact. Telling George here that you're coming to live with me when you get back from Melbourne.'

'George?'

'My new gardener. Marvellous man. Strong and hardy, like a plant himself. He said you sounded nice too. He's surprisingly knowledgeable about all sorts of things, not only plants. Quite the antiques expert. Says

I'm sitting on some valuable objects here. I'm not surprised. Vincent had a wonderful eye.'

An alarm bell rang. 'Mill, who is this George?'

'George. Of George's Gorgeous Gardens. He's perfectly legitimate. Large ad in the Yellow Pages. A website even, he tells me. Not that I'm too sure what that is.'

Sylvie decided she'd check it out as soon as possible. But in the meantime . . .

'Mill, please don't tell people I'm coming to live with you.'

'You want to keep it a secret? No problem at all. I was saying to George that the blue room is definitely the best one for you, but he said we might get bats in the Moreton Bay out the front, or even the occasional funnel web. You wouldn't mind them, would you? You don't look the squeamish, timid type to me.'

'Mill, I don't know how to make this any clearer, but I'm not planning on coming back to Sydney for a while. Possibly ever. I'm looking for work here.'

'I understand completely. Just let me know when you're due back and I'll get someone to meet you at the airport. Now, I'd better give you today's tip. When you're frying eggs, sprinkle a little bit of flour in the hot oil. It stops any spatters. Bye for now, Sylvie.'

That hadn't gone right, Sylvie thought, looking down at the phone. The call had warmed her up, though. Before there was time to think, she took out the piece of paper with Max's number on it and dialled.

It rang six times before a man answered. Was it him? She didn't know his voice well enough. 'Max?'

'Sylvie, I was just thinking about you.'

'You were?'

'I was going to ring and ask if you wanted to meet me for a drink at the end of the week.'

Drat, he'd got in first. She needed to ask him out on a date. Did it count that she was the one who had rung him?

'Sylvie, are you there? I've asked you for a drink, not a round-the-world cruise. Just say yes.'

The laughter in his voice gave her nerve. 'Max, I'm sorry, but can you hang up and then answer it again when I ring?'

'I could, if you truly think that makes any sense.'

'I'll explain why later.'

'I'll look forward to that.' He hung up.

She dialled the number again. 'Max?'

'Sylvie, hello. Who'd have thought? How are you today?' He sounded like a detective trying to talk a mad person off a window ledge.

'Would you like to meet me for a drink on Friday night?'

'What a lovely idea. I wish I'd thought of it myself.'

She crossed the dare off the list. 'Thank you very much. Seven o'clock? The Spanish bar? Great, see you then.'

She hung up. She felt great. Really great. And not only because she'd already done one of her dares.

There was a knock at the front door just after three o'clock. It was Leila. She didn't waste time with pleasantries. 'That coffee you mentioned the other day. I don't suppose it's still up for grabs?'

'Of course, come in. How did it go?'

'The soap audition? It was disastrous.'

'What happened?'

'Self-sabotage.' Leila gave a big sigh as she followed Sylvie into the kitchen. 'Something got into me about two minutes after I arrived and I couldn't stop giggling. Which would have been fine if it had been a girly part, but I was going for the part of a newly widowed young mother. I read the lines as if it was the most hilarious thing that had ever happened to me.'

'Oh, Leila.'

'"Oh, Leila" is right. And do you know what made it worse? I heard them talking about it afterwards. They said it was the worst audition they'd ever seen. The producer said that one is definitely going on the bloopers tape. I don't blame them. You should have seen me. "*He's dead? My husband's dead? But how will I go on without him?*" And me laughing as if I've inhaled a hot-air balloon full of laughing gas.'

'It must have been nerves.'

'Not nerves. The gods telling me to find a new career. Sylvie, do you have any cigarettes?'

'Sorry, no. I don't smoke.'

'Neither do I. I want to start, though. Forget the coffee. Do you have to do anything today? Will you come and get drunk with me? You didn't have anything else planned, did you?'

Sylvie thought of Sebastian's list. 'Actually, yes. A dinner party. For next Saturday night. Would you like to come?'

'Sure. If you come and get drunk with me now.'

'It's a deal.'

Six hours later, it took Sylvie five tries to get her key in the lock. It was nearly midnight. Her head was spinning from too much vodka, too much loud music and eight unaccustomed cigarettes. She squinted as she looked at the answering machine. No messages from Mill tonight. Oh, God. That reminded her. She'd meant to check the George's Gorgeous Gardens website. Some great-niece she was. Mill could be cut up in tiny pieces and buried under the flagstones of her newly gorgeous garden by now.

As she waited for Sebastian's computer to warm up, Sylvie went to the kitchen and made herself drink three large glasses of water. She caught sight of her reflection in the dark of the kitchen window. A panda looked back at her. She always ended up with mascara smudges under her eyes when she laughed. She'd spent most of the afternoon laughing.

'What Midas is to gold, I am to chaos,' Leila had announced as they walked to a bar she knew in Prahran. 'Everything I touch turns to ruin. I'm the original Calamity Jane. It's not funny, Sylvie. Stop smiling. I can't help it. I've been like it since I was a child.'

As they played pool, Leila entertained her with a litany of her disasters. Her first cubby-house, built by her farmer father in secret for her tenth birthday, swept away in a flash flood the day after her party. Her first day at high school ruined when she spent the day with her school uniform tucked into her knickers. Her step into independence, moving to Melbourne from a country town north of Ballarat as a twenty-eight-year-old, hitting a major road-hump when the removal van carrying all her belongings caught fire en route. Her attempt to stave off loneliness in her first few months by volunteering to visit old people in their homes coming to an end when her allocated old lady sacked her for not being interesting enough. Her attempt to get fit ending in failure when her clothes were stolen from the side of the Harold Holt pool while she was swimming laps one winter afternoon. She'd had to catch the tram home wearing only her bathers.

'That's why it's good to hang around me,' Leila had said. 'I attract everybody else's share of bad luck as well as my own. Do you think I could hire myself out? As a kind of reverse good-luck charm?'

Still smiling at the memory, Sylvie carried a fourth glass of water into Sebastian's office. The computer rippled into life. After one or two vodka-fuelled spelling mistakes, she found the website for George's Gorgeous Gardens. It was professional, with photographs, a detailed profile of George himself, a long list of his qualifications. There were more than a dozen testimonials from happy clients. Good. It looked like Mill, and her garden, were in safe hands. Safe green thumbs, even.

In bed soon after, trying to get to sleep and ignore her spinning head, Sylvie remembered something else Leila had said that day. Something that didn't make her smile.

They'd been in the third bar of the day, playing their fourth game of pool, drinking their third or possibly fourth vodka and tonic. Sylvie had told Leila about the treasure hunt Sebastian had left, the clues leading to the bookshop and the list of dares. Pressed for more details, she'd told her about the situation with her mother and sisters in Sydney, and all that had happened the night of Vanessa's wedding.

'I wish I had a big brother who cared about me like that,' Leila said. 'My three little brothers are demons.

Heavy metal music-lovers. Motorbike-addicts. If there's ever an earthquake in Victoria, the epicentre will be our house.' She expertly potted three balls, then looked across the green table.

'Where's your father, Sylvie? You haven't mentioned him.'

'Here. In Melbourne.'

'They're divorced?'

Sylvie nodded.

'What happened?'

'Irreconcilable differences. Is that the legal term for screaming at each other all the time? He left when I was eight. Sebastian went with him.'

'Have you seen your dad since you've been down here?'

'I haven't seen him since I was eight.'

Leila stopped lining up her shot. 'Twenty years?'

'Twenty-one.'

'Why not?'

'Mum didn't want me to when I was younger. It would upset her too much if I suggested it. And since then . . .' She shrugged.

'Aren't you curious? Even to have a look at him?'

What she felt wasn't curiosity. It was hurt, wrapped up in years of no phone calls or birthday cards. 'It's too late now. And I still wouldn't like to upset Mum.' It sounded feeble even to her own ears.

'But you're an adult female. Your role in life as a daughter is to upset your mother. Didn't you know that? I drive my mother bananas.'

'It's more complicated than that.'

'You must be curious, though?'

Sylvie wanted to drop this topic. 'Of course. But he's always known where I was as well. It takes two.'

'I disagree. It takes one. One of you to make the first move.' They played two shots each before Leila spoke again. 'Can I ask you a blunt question?'

In Sylvie's experience, the best answer to an enquiry like that was usually no. 'Go ahead.'

'Have you ever thought about taking charge of your own life?'

'Pardon?'

Leila chalked the end of her cue, looking seriously over at Sylvie. 'I'm sorry if this comes out wrong, but the way you've told it, you've spent the past few years doing whatever your mother and sisters told you to do. Now you're down here doing what Sebastian wants you to do. Not just coming to Melbourne and minding his house, but this whole treasure hunt thing.'

'It's only a bit of fun.'

'I know. And I told you, I'd love a big brother who did something like this for me. But you're nearly thirty. When are you going to start making your own decisions? About life. About seeing your father. You're

79

obviously bright, you're great company. I can't see why you haven't broken out on your own before now.'

Sylvie couldn't tell whether Leila was insulting or complimenting her. 'I haven't been sure what I wanted to do yet.'

'No? Fair enough.' Leila lined up the ball, played her shot. It missed. 'It's probably easier to let other people boss you around, then. Your turn, Sylvie.'

Leila's words kept going around her head. Is that what she'd been doing? Taking the easy way out by letting people boss her around? She hoped not. Wasn't it that she liked helping people? Being busy? Feeling needed? Or had she let it become an excuse?

It was past three before she got to sleep.

She rang her mother first thing the next morning, before she made coffee or tried to find some headache tablets. If she kept waiting for her to call, it might never happen. If she wanted to talk to her mother, then it was up to her to ring.

Fidelma sounded genuinely delighted to hear from her. 'Sylvie, darling, how are things? I was leaving you alone. You have enough of me in Sydney. I thought you might like the peace. Ray and I are back from the retreat and I feel truly inspired. I've already got ideas for my next exhibition. I do believe the landscape there speaks right to my inner self. Ray was up before dawn each morning meditating, and he agrees that being close to nature is so important, not just for our creativity but for our souls. I'm thinking of introducing a new element to my work, possibly multimedia, incorporating . . .'

When she hung up ten minutes later, Sylvie realised her mother had never actually heard how things were going for her in Melbourne or how she was feeling. Either Sylvie was still numb from all the vodka the day before, or she didn't mind as much as usual.

As she went out for a walk a little later her eyes were drawn once again to her father's photograph in the hallway. She stopped and looked at it.

What would they talk about if she did ring him? His poetry? The truth was she'd never really understood it. It was experimental, jagged, angry writing. What else had Sebastian said about him? That he spoke Swahili? Lived in a penthouse? Drove a new car? Or maybe none of those things?

It would be easy to find out. All she had to do was ring Sebastian and ask for her father's contact number. Get his address. Turn up on his doorstep and say, 'Hello, Dad. I'm your daughter.'

But what would happen then, she wondered. Where did you start with someone you hadn't seen for twenty-one years?

Leila didn't bother knocking when she called by later that afternoon.

'Are you dying of a hangover?' she called out. 'It's your own fault if you are. You should have said no when I asked you to come out with me.'

'I'm telling myself the same thing,' Sylvie said, looking up from her nest of cushions in the bay window. An empty can of Coke and bag of chips was beside her. 'I think it would be dangerous to be your friend.'

'That's why I don't have any friends. That, and my bad habit of speaking my mind. I do remember that right, don't I? I did tell you to get a grip on your own life last night?'

'You did, yes.'

'And I've only just met you. And I don't know the whole story. And who am I to tell you, with my own life a mess. That's what you thought, didn't you?'

'You're a mind reader as well as an actress?'

'A failed actress. Please use the correct terminology. Sorry, Sylvie. That was out of line of me. I was right, of course, but it wasn't my job to tell you.'

Sylvie liked Leila too much to be mad at her. And there was also the little matter of Leila possibly hitting the nail on the head . . . 'You're forgiven, I promise. Can I get you back, though? I'm meeting a friend for a drink on Friday night. Do you want to come along too?'

'How can you have another friend already? You've only just arrived in Melbourne. That's not fair. I've been here nearly two years and I hardly know anyone.'

'He's a friend of Seb's.'

'That brother of yours knows too many people. I can't come, as it turns out. I'm having dinner with friends in Carlton.'

'So you do have friends?'

'Only ones who feel sorry for me. I met this couple when I was doing some house-sitting last summer. I managed to set their chimney on fire. I know. Don't ask. But thanks anyway.'

'You're welcome. And thanks for last night.'

'Thanks for the hangover, you mean.' Leila gave her a cheery wave and a smile as she headed out again. 'See, I really am a mind reader!'

CHAPTER SEVEN

Sylvie was woken two mornings later by the sound of the phone ringing. Not Mill, but one of the temp agencies she'd registered with. They had a job for her that day. A firm called Dennison Reilly. Data entry. She scribbled down the address. St Kilda Road, twenty minutes' walk from Sebastian's apartment. Yes, she'd love to take it. Be there at eight thirty? No problem at all.

It felt good to be in work clothes again, instead of the jeans and T-shirts she'd been living in the past week or so. She looked the image of efficiency, pencil skirt, crisp white shirt, pearl earrings and black pumps. She'd called into a hairdresser on Toorak Road the previous afternoon and had one of her best cuts in years. The corkscrew curls were now soft waves, close to her head. Gamine, the hairdresser told her. Whatever it was called, it had been easy to manage that morning.

She arrived at the large, glass-clad twenty-storey building on St Kilda Road at eight twenty a.m. She had to sign in, then wait with fifteen other corporately clad people to be taken up seventeen floors to a warren of silent offices. A middle-aged woman came to the reception desk to collect Sylvie. Dark hair pulled back in a ponytail. A lot of makeup. A strong floral perfume. She didn't offer her name, or make any small chat.

Sylvie tried her best as she followed her along the corridor. 'You have a great view from up here.'

No answer.

'You're an insurance company, I believe?' She'd glanced at the brochures in the reception area.

The woman gave a nod.

Sylvie was shown to a small, windowless cubicle with a computer and five boxes of files. The supervisor didn't meet her eye once. She could have been showing a trained monkey around. She gestured to the computer, where a database was already up on screen. 'Update those files. Check the details against the files in that box.' She pointed again and then turned to leave.

'Please,' Sylvie said, with a bright smile.

There was eye contact then. 'What?'

It felt important to say something. 'I'm sorry, but I felt like you were telling me, not asking me.'

'I am telling you, not asking you. You're a temp.'

The woman left her then, shutting the door with

something close to a slam behind her. After a moment wondering whether to curse or laugh, Sylvie made a start on the work. Compared to all the years with Executive Stress Relief, not to mention her time in the family studio, this felt like taking baby steps. Routine, repetitive and strangely restful. Her fingers flew across the keyboard as she rapidly input the information. She did a quick calculation. The temp agency might not be pleased commission-wise, but she could probably get through most of these files today.

Fifteen minutes later, Sylvie got a phone call. It was the agency.

'We've had a complaint, Sylvie. I'm surprised, because your references from Sydney were so excellent.'

'What kind of complaint?'

'You apparently have an attitude problem.'

'I do?'

'Our client said you were insolent and showed a lack of respect. She also reminded me, as I'll also tell you, that they are one of our best customers.'

There was no point going into it then. 'I'm sorry,' Sylvie said. 'I certainly didn't mean to be insolent.'

'Work through to lunchtime, would you? I'll send another temp in this afternoon.'

'You're taking me off the job?'

'She's asked us to. Demanded it.'

'That's fine,' Sylvie said calmly, outwardly professional,

inwardly swearing. 'I'll keep working in the meantime.'

She got through almost a box of files by eleven thirty, before she realised she needed a coffee and a bathroom. The woman hadn't shown her where either was. Sylvie made her way down the corridor, peering into the offices. There was little chat, just heads down working. She found the woman at the end of the building, standing by the coffee machine.

'You're still here?' Not a hello, not a 'Can I help you?'

'Just until lunchtime,' Sylvie said, trying to keep her voice and expression pleasant. 'I needed a coffee. Can I please help myself?'

The woman stepped to one side, still blocking the cups. 'Five minutes break, maximum.'

Sylvie made a coffee, pressing the buttons, watching the dart of instant coffee arrive in the cup. She thought of all the temp jobs she'd had, all the other temps she'd met, the different experiences of the job that she'd heard about. She remembered how well treated and respected she was by the Executive Stress Relief clients. As the other woman threw her empty cup into the bin and turned to leave, Sylvie seized her moment.

'Excuse me?'

The woman stopped.

'I hope you don't mind me saying, but I think you might be the one with the attitude problem here.'

'What?'

'Temps are human beings too. Not robots. I wasn't being insolent, I was asking to be treated with some respect and –'

'That's enough. Your five minutes break is up. I hope you don't mind me saying.' The last was delivered in a sarcastic tone.

Sylvie was barely back in her cubicle when she got another phone call from the agency.

'She's asked for you to be removed now. We've got your replacement coming in urgently. We'll have to take you off our books, Sylvie. We can't have a loose cannon working for us.'

A loose cannon? Her? It felt like the biggest compliment she'd ever been paid. 'I understand completely,' she said.

Her bravado had faded by the time she walked home. Her shoes were pinching. Her shirt was sticking to her back. It was an unseasonally warm day. It didn't bode well for her future here in Melbourne if she was sacked from her first job.

The phone in the hallway was ringing as she let herself in. 'Sebastian's house.'

'Sylvie, I didn't expect to get you. I have another tip for you. Do you have paper and a pen?'

'Of course, Mill.' She reached into her bag for a notebook. 'Ready when you are.'

'You sound quite flat. Not yourself at all. What's wrong? Has something happened?'

'It has, yes.' Sylvie was surprised to hear herself say it. 'Just something silly.'

'It's the silly things that are often the most upsetting, in my experience. Tell me. I've been on my own in the house all day. I could do with a story.'

Sylvie told Mill everything that had happened in the insurance office. 'I keep wishing I'd said something else to her. Told the agency what she was like. I shouldn't have let her get away with it.'

'No, you shouldn't have,' Mill said. 'You should have set fire to all her files before you left.'

Sylvie laughed. 'Exactly. And then wiped out the computer program.'

'Yes. Then dialled the speaking clock in China on the office phone. Put a prawn inside her curtain rod. Let down her tyres. Offered her some laxative chocolates. Sprinkled itching powder in her hair.'

'They're not more of your handy household hints, are they?'

Mill laughed enthusiastically. 'No, but wouldn't it be fun to try them one day? I'm glad you're out of there, Sylvie. That woman sounds like a horrible stinking old bitch.'

'Mill!'

'Well, she does. I can't abide bullying behaviour.

People trying to put others in their place. It's a sign of insecurity, you know. Something similar happened to me when I was your age. This particular gentleman used to turn up his nose at me when I would attend recitals with Vincent. "I don't know what he's doing out socially with his housekeeper," he said to me once. Looked down his nose. It's an apt expression, that one. So I lifted my chin one night and said, "I'm sensational in bed, as it happens." That shut him up. Though of course it went around like wildfire that I wasn't a housekeeper but some kind of a prostitute. Vincent thought it was hilarious. Would tell people he'd bought me on hire purchase.' She went off into peals of laughter.

'Mill, have you been drinking?'

'At this time of day, of course not. Cocktail hour is six p.m. Why do you young people assume we never had sex in our day? Surry Hills was as much a hotbed back then as it is now. Vincent was quite adventurous too, you know. He loved it when I –'

'Mill, please.'

'Oh, how marvellous. George has pulled up outside. He said he'd try and drop by today, even for a few minutes. He's doing wonders. Quite transforming the garden. Once you and I get started on the inside it'll be a whole new place. Did I give you today's tip, by the way?'

'No, not yet.'

'Cold cream. It's all a woman needs for her skin. That and a hat to keep the sun off. Speak to you soon, Sylvie.'

'Thanks, Mill –' It was too late. She'd already hung up.

Sylvie made a cup of tea, thought about it for a little while, and then rang the woman at the temp agency. She told her exactly what had happened with the client that morning. She spoke calmly and authoritatively. The woman listened, asked several questions and then apologised. She hadn't realised the client was treating staff like that, she said. She asked if Sylvie wanted to stay on their books. Thank you, but no, Sylvie said.

Someone had tried to call while she was talking to the agency. She pressed play on the answering machine. A familiar voice filled the hallway.

'Sylvie, it's Jill from Executive Stress Relief in Sydney calling. It's short notice, I know, but would you be free to meet me for lunch on Monday?' A soft laugh. 'In Melbourne, of course. I'm going to be down there for a couple of days. I'd love to meet up.' Brisk and to the point, as she always was.

Sylvie called back immediately. Jill had just gone into a meeting. Sylvie spoke to her assistant. Arrangements were made to meet at a French bistro at Southgate.

Perfect. She couldn't wait. And the irony was if she hadn't been sacked from her first temp job in Melbourne, she wouldn't have been free to meet Jill.

She took off her horrible work pumps and did a stockinged-foot slide across the floor in celebration.

That night Sylvie spent an hour on Sebastian's computer, researching tips for successful dinner parties. Hers was all organised for the following Saturday. She'd rung and invited Max and Donald as well. They'd both accepted.

She'd decided on an Asian banquet. Several different starters and main courses, a symphony of taste sensations, according to the recipe books she'd consulted. She decided against a practice run. She knew how to cook, after all. And cooking with exotic ingredients was the same as cooking with ordinary ingredients. A matter of following steps, being organised, getting the timing right.

There were plenty of helpful websites. Sylvie soon had a list of tips on table settings, cocktails and serving etiquette, as well as possible witty conversation topics and after-dinner word games. She was about to log off when a bright sound heralded the arrival of an email. She clicked on it without thinking.

From: LaurenceDevereaux@hotmail.com

To: SebastianDevereaux@yahoo.com

Re: Dinner?

Seb, dinner Friday fortnight? Booking made. Will see you there unless I hear back to the contrary. Dad

She read it four times. At this exact moment, somewhere in Melbourne, her father was sitting at his computer. If she wanted to, she could write back immediately. Hi Dad, it's your daughter Sylvie. Long time no hear!

She was tempted, for one moment. Her fingers hovered over the keyboard. Then she disconnected and closed the computer down. She sent Sebastian a text telling him about the email, and apologising for opening it. That was all she needed to do with it.

Chapter Eight

'You're doing wonders for my social life, Sylvie,' Max said. 'Two nights out and an invitation to a dinner party. You're spoiling me.'

They were in the Spanish bar together again. Outside, the weather had turned bad, rain pelting down, the gutters rushing with water. Inside it was warm and cosy, the lights low, the background guitar music swirling around them. There were tapas plates and a nearly empty bottle of wine in front of them. The room was almost full, end of the week chatter all around.

'You have Sebastian to thank, really,' she said. 'His dares, at least.'

'Am I that scary? That he had to dare you to ask me out?'

'Very scary.'

'How fantastic. I've been striking fear into the hearts

of people without being aware of it. Was it my latent masculinity? My powerful voice? My manly aura?'

'All those things, definitely.'

'Are you still scared?'

'Not any more.'

'So this is actually a date, not a drink? And I arrived here so innocently.'

'Not really.' Embarrassed, she backtracked. 'It was a dare to ask someone out on a date. Not you, specifically.' That sounded even worse. 'I didn't know anyone else to ask.' Worse still.

Max didn't seem hurt. 'I'm happy for you to practise on me. As long as I'm not ruining your chances with someone else. You haven't left anyone pining in Sydney?'

'You can't hear that howling? All the forlorn boyfriends I've left behind?' She shook her head. 'No, there's no one in Sydney.' A pause. 'And you?'

'No one in Sydney for me either. Or in Melbourne. Or in Adelaide, Perth, Hobart, Canberra, Brisbane or Darwin. There was a brief flirtation with someone in Wagga Wagga, or was it Coolangatta? Alas, it didn't work out between us. I'm footloose and fancy free. No, to be accurate, footloose, fancy free and scary.'

'I'm sorry to disappoint you, but you're really not scary at all.'

'I'm not? Good.' He smiled across the table at her.

Four hours later he was sitting close beside her, speaking into her ear. They were in a small jazz and blues club he liked, off Chapel Street in Prahran. The music was so loud it was the only way they could make themselves heard. She'd been telling him about Aunt Mill's phone calls.

'Are you actually keeping a record of these handy household hints?'

'I am, though I don't know what I'll do with them.' She'd told Max the ones she remembered. He said he was definitely going to try the linen and denture tablets tip.

'Mill's the one who asked you to be her companion?' he asked.

Sebastian had obviously told him everything. She nodded. 'She was housekeeper to this musician, Vincent Langan, and when he died he left –'

'Vincent Langan?' Max's shout coincided with the end of a song. Several people turned around. 'The jazz composer?'

'You've heard of him?'

'Of course I've heard of him. He was an absolute legend in the Sydney jazz scene in the fifties. Incredible. Completely under-rated since. Did you actually know him?'

'I only met him once. At a family gathering.'

'Oh, God. I wouldn't have minded meeting him at a

funeral. An abattoir open day. He didn't play anything that day, did he? Talk about his music?'

Sylvie shook her head.

Max made an elaborate show of touching her hand. 'I can't believe it. It's like that song, I danced with the girl who danced with the man who danced with the Prince of Wales.' He laughed. 'Or however it goes. Wait till I tell my friends I've spent the evening with the woman whose great-aunt was the housekeeper to Vincent Langan.'

He was half joking, Sylvie knew, but she suddenly sobered up. It was David all over again. Liked for her family, not for herself. She stood up. 'Max, I'm really sorry, but I need to head home. Can I get you a drink before I go?'

'Just like that? Are you okay?'

'A bad headache,' she lied. 'And toothache.'

'Headache and toothache? Together?'

It did sound suspicious. 'I'm prone to them unfortunately.'

'What did I say, Sylvie? I've upset you somehow.'

'Nothing. It's just a toothache. And headache.'

'Let me walk you home.'

'It's raining. I'll get a taxi.'

'If you're sure.'

'I'm sure.' She saw his expression change. He'd picked up every signal she was hurling at him. She was saying 'back away' and he was backing away. She felt a shimmer of regret. More than that. All evening she'd been finding him more and more attractive.

He became businesslike too. 'If you feel like calling off the dinner party, if your toothache is too bad –'

She'd forgotten all about the dinner party. She'd see that dare through, then the fun and games were over. 'Of course not,' she said, hating the false tone in her voice. 'I'll be fine once I get some painkillers. I'll see you next Saturday.'

'It was a great night tonight. Thanks a lot. I hope you feel better soon.'

'Thanks. See you.'

Ten minutes later, as she sat in the back of the taxi, rain pelting against the windows, she waited for the feeling of certainty to arrive, the knowledge that she'd made the right decision leaving when she did. That she'd been right to stand up for herself. Right not to let what happened with David happen again with Max.

The certainty didn't arrive. All that did was a sinking feeling she'd just spoilt something good.

It was a relief on Monday to be sitting with her old boss Jill over lunch. Familiar, businesslike. All that was different was they were in Melbourne, with the Yarra in the background instead of Sydney Harbour. Jill always ate in waterside restaurants. She told Sylvie the food tasted better.

Jill laughed as Sylvie told her of her first Melbourne temp experience.

'That will teach you to punch beneath your weight. What are you doing wasting your talents on data entry? You could have been running a place like that.'

'It's a deliberate approach. My slow takeover of Melbourne's office scene. Start at the bottom and work my way up.'

'Or you could start at the top.'

'Sorry?'

'You know I'm not one to mince my words, Sylvie. I'm not here on holiday. I'm here for business and to see you. Which is also business.'

Sylvie waited.

'An opportunity has come up for us to buy out an existing recruitment agency here. I want to start a Melbourne branch of Executive Stress Relief. Same principles, same philosophy, on a small scale to begin with. A sub-branch of the main recruitment business, if you like, targeting high-level clients. You know how it works. I want you to think about taking it on for me.'

'Managing it?'

'From day one. It would be your project.' Jill named an excellent salary. She mentioned a car. Rental assistance. An expense account.

'But why me?'

'You're the best person for the job. You've already proved yourself workwise, many times over. You also showed get up and go, moving down here the way you did.'

If only Jill knew. Sylvie kept her mouth shut.

'Will you think about it?' Jill said. 'I need an answer by the end of next week.'

'I'll definitely think about it.'

Jill held up her glass. 'To our business partnership?'

'To our business partnership,' Sylvie echoed.

CHAPTER NINE

Less than an hour into her dinner party, Sylvie knew she'd made a big mistake.

On the surface, all was perfect. The living room looked like the inside of a jewellery box. She'd turned the lights down low, sending a soft glow onto the golden drapes. Mellow background music was playing. She'd pushed the sofas to the edge of the room and moved the antique dining table and four chairs into the centre. With the food having an Asian theme, she'd set the table to match – serviettes folded into elegant origami swan shapes (she'd found the instructions on the Internet), chopsticks resting on elegant ceramic holders on a richly patterned tablecloth. Four low candles completed the look.

Throughout her preparations, she'd thought long and hard about Max and her reaction to his comments about

Vincent Langan. Her overreaction. Max had been paying for Evil David's sins, she realised. She hadn't been fair on him. He was obviously a genuine fan of Vincent Langan's music, he'd had every right to be excited at the idea of Sylvie having met him. She'd decided to apologise to him as soon as she had the opportunity. And if he wanted it, she would give him Great-Aunt Mill's phone number. She knew Mill would love to talk about Vincent to anyone who cared to hear about him.

Max, Leila and Donald arrived within minutes of each other, just after seven thirty. Sylvie had been dressed and made-up since before six thirty, wearing a black top and cardigan, dark-orange skirt and her favourite high peep-toe shoes, which lifted her height to a towering five foot four.

Her guests had dressed up too. Leila had wound her long red hair into a loose bun and made up her eyes in an exotic way. She was wearing a close-fitting red velvet vintage dress, showing lots of cleavage.

Donald was wearing a grey suit, white shirt and red tie, understated but elegant. He seemed at home in Sebastian's apartment, hanging up his coat, standing beside Sylvie and taking Max and Leila's coats as they arrived too. He'd kissed Sylvie's cheek as he came in. She'd wondered whether to say something, to whisper, 'I know about you and Sebastian and I heartily approve,' as she gave him a kiss back. She decided against it.

Max was wearing a dark-green smoking jacket over old-fashioned suit trousers. All borrowed from his flatmate's grandfather, he announced. 'I was thinking Gabriel Byrne in *Miller's Crossing*,' he said. 'But it's more bit part in *Bugsy Malone*, isn't it?'

Sylvie served champagne cocktails to begin. She felt like an actress in a 1940s comedy, laughing over her shoulder as she dropped sugar cubes into the tall glasses and the champagne fizzed and bubbled up the side of the glass. She'd been worried there would be awkward silences, but there wasn't a moment's lapse in conversation. Donald talked about a forthcoming author visit to his bookshop. It sparked a childhood anecdote from Leila about meeting her favourite writer and being sick on his shoes in excitement. Max told a story about a customer coming into the store, looking around and asking, 'Are these books for sale?'

Sylvie excused herself after serving another round of cocktails. Seb's kitchen was down a small hallway from the living room, not ideal for entertaining but she could still hear the conversations, at least. She'd banned them from coming into the kitchen. She didn't want anyone seeing her military-style preparations. Six of Sebastian's Asian cookbooks were arranged on the shelves. In front of each relevant recipe were the ingredients she needed. She had a running-order pinned on the wall beside the noticeboard.

The smells were glorious, spring onions, garlic, ginger, coriander, basil, sesame oil. She had spent nearly three hours at the Queen Vic food market, roaming the aisles, browsing the different stalls, revelling in having the time to do it. In Sydney, working full-time, it had been a matter of running into the nearest supermarket after work, grabbing whatever ingredients Fidelma was eating at the time and cooking them in simple ways – steaming, grilling or baking.

She wished she'd taken that approach now. Why hadn't she read the directions more clearly? Noticed each recipe had preparation times varying from thirty minutes to one hour, even if the cooking time in the wok was just a minute or two? How on earth did Chinese, Thai and Vietnamese restaurants manage to serve anybody, let alone so quickly? By having a team of cooks, of course. And more than one wok.

When in doubt, open another bottle of wine. 'Not long now,' she announced, putting another bottle of red on the table. They had already finished the first one.

They were halfway through the second bottle by the time she appeared with the starters: grilled prawns with coriander, lemongrass and ginger; and stir-fried calamari with garlic, celery and shallots. If they noticed the prawns were a little wan-looking from sitting in the oven keeping warm while she stir-fried the calamari, they didn't say. She was showered in compliments. If only the cooking ended there. She thought of the other ten bowls of ingredients waiting to be cooked for the main courses. Was it too late to order in a pizza?

The last prawn was on the plate, being argued over, when Donald's mobile rang. It was the security firm who monitored the bookshop. The alarm had been triggered. They'd checked, it looked secure, but they needed him to come down.

'I'll go,' Max said. 'You've worked back late all week.'

Donald was already folding his serviette. 'No. I don't pay you enough to do overtime. I'll take a look. I'll be back as soon as I can.'

He rang fifteen minutes later. There'd been an attempted break-in. The window into the storeroom was broken. He needed to wait for the glazier. 'I'm sorry, Sylvie.'

'It's fine. Do you want me to save some for you? I can drop it around tomorrow.'

'That would be lovely.'

The evening changed from that moment. As Sylvie worked in the kitchen, chopping up more spring onions and garlic, measuring more sesame oil, soy sauce and rice wine, she heard laughing. She heard Leila tell stories of disastrous auditions she'd done. Max saying she should forget about being a serious actor and turn her stories into a stand-up comedy routine. Leila laughingly dismissing him and telling another one.

Max saying, 'Seriously, why don't you think about it? I'll help you.'

'Help me?'

'Sure. Help you rehearse it. Stage it. There's open mike spots in the comedy clubs all around town.'

'You're serious.'

'Deadly serious. Funny serious too.'

By the time Sylvie began bringing the main course dishes in (stir-fried mussels with black bean and chilli, crispy chicken in garlic-ginger sauce, and beef in spicy coconut milk), Max and Leila had struck a mother lode of shared interests. Comedians they'd seen. Actors they admired. Plays they'd read. As Sylvie delivered the side dishes of rice and choy sum with oyster sauce, she realised she'd become a waitress in her own home.

They'd barely finished eating when Max said, 'One of the clubs off Chapel Street has a late-night stand-up slot.' He checked his watch. 'Starting in about half an hour.'

Sylvie knew it was up to her. If she insisted they stay, she'd feel guilty. She also knew it would take her a little while to prepare the dessert. Fresh fruit salad in cointreau, served with vanilla ice-cream. She hadn't cut up the fruit yet. She pulled a big smile from somewhere.

'What a fantastic idea,' she said. 'It was only going to be fruit for dessert. We could eat an apple each on the way.'

Max and Leila laughed uproariously. She realised she was about five glasses of wine behind them.

Within minutes of arriving at the comedy club, she knew she should have stayed home. In years to come, if she ever met Max and Leila's children, she would be able to tell them she was there the night they met and could report it had practically been love at first sight. They hadn't just hit it off. They'd slammed it off. There was so much electricity zipping back and forth between them Sylvie expected her hair to stand on end.

Neither of them seemed concerned when she made a show of looking at her watch at twelve thirty. 'Do you mind if I head off?'

'Of course not.'

'You must be exhausted after all that cooking.'

'Thanks for a great night, Sylvie.'

'Really great. Fantastic food.'

She wondered if they'd even noticed what they were eating.

Leila gave her a flamboyant two-cheek kiss goodbye. Max hugged her. He felt good, as she'd expected he would. Something was missing, though. The promise of something. Whatever had been between them was gone, transferred in Leila's direction. She hadn't mentioned his comment about Vincent Langan, or apologised for her reaction. There seemed no reason to, now. She suddenly felt stone cold sober. Not only that. Foolish and sad, as well.

They were both back engrossed in their conversation before she reached the exit.

The next morning Sylvie was woken by a knock at the door. She checked the bedside clock. Ten a.m. It was Leila. She looked like she'd been lit from inside. 'I know it's early, but I'm dying to talk. Can I come in?'

She was in and curled up on the sofa before Sylvie knew what had happened, like a cat on a wet winter evening.

'Sylvie, that was the best night ever. I have to thank you so much. Not only dinner. But for –'

'Introducing you to Max?'

Leila put her arms around herself in a hug. 'I'm in love, Sylvie. I swear it. It's like we've known each other all our lives. He's so funny. So sweet. I can't believe I haven't met him before. Thank God you came down. If it wasn't for you, I –' Sylvie knew her expression had given her away when Leila suddenly clapped her hand over her mouth. 'Oh, God. Oh, God. There wasn't something between you, was there? And I've blundered in? Oh, Sylvie.'

'Of course not. I only just met him.' She was a better actress than Leila, she hoped. 'That's great you got on so well. So what did you get up to after I left?'

They'd stayed in the comedy club until it closed. Gone

on to a late-night bar in the city centre. He'd walked her home at five a.m.

'And you're seeing him again?' Sylvie's voice was studiedly casual.

'Tonight. We were thinking about going for a drink. Or I might give him a call and see if he wants to go and see some more comedy.' A too-long pause. 'Would you like to come along?'

'No, I'm busy tonight, but thanks anyway.' A bright smile. 'So, can I get you a coffee?'

The first two dares were done. She rang Sebastian with her report.

'I did enjoy my date with Max, thank you very much. The dinner party was pretty much a disaster, unfortunately. But I'm pleased to tell you your informal matchmaking plans worked a treat.'

'You and Max got together? Excellent!'

'Not me and Max. Max and Leila.'

'Max and *Leila*? Bloody hell.'

Sylvie had to laugh at the surprise in his voice. 'They've got a lot in common. Comedy, theatre . . .'

'I'm still surprised. I thought Leila would be too daft for Max. Shows how much I know.'

'She told me she's in love.'

'Leila falls in love every second week. Well, good luck

to them, but I still think you were the better match. And you haven't finished the dares, by the way. Check the form. I want you to do one more for me.'

'Swim the length of the Yarra in a duck costume?'

'A little easier than that. I can't make dinner with Dad after all. I need you to go in my place.'

'Very funny.' Her heart started beating faster.

'Please, Sylvie. It would be bad manners if he turned up and I wasn't there.'

'Can't you ring and tell him you can't make it?'

'I think it's a good opportunity for you to meet him. And I want you to meet him.'

'More matchmaking? It hasn't worked out so far.' She hoped to deflect him with a joke. She also hoped he couldn't hear the note of panic in her voice.

'He's your father, Sylvie. He's not getting any younger. All I'm asking is you have dinner with him. In return for letting you stay in my house rent free. And yes, I know that's blackmail.'

'It's not blackmail, it's bullying.'

'I've been waiting for you to ask me for his contact number. I didn't want to force it on you. But not a word out of you about him. And I think it's important.'

'He's known I'm here, too. Have I had a message from him? An invitation to meet up? No.'

'Sylvie, he's got a lot on his plate. Complicated things. It's harder for him.'

She was surprised at her sudden anger. 'And it's easy for me?'

'Easier, yes. I think it is.' Silence for a moment. 'Please, Sylvie. Just go. And I don't think I should let him know it's you instead of me. If it's a surprise, he won't get too anxious beforehand –'

'He's had some sort of a breakdown? Is that what you're hinting at?'

'No, he hasn't had a breakdown. But all of this has been hard for him too. There's pride involved. Guilt. Try and understand.'

'How can I understand him? I don't know him.'

'So here's your chance. A starting point. A nice meal in a good restaurant, a couple of glasses of wine. It might be the best way to do it.'

Sylvie stayed silent. She pictured it. Pictured herself arriving at the restaurant. Seeing her father across the room. Walking over to him . . . Her heart started thumping again.

'Sylvie? Yes, no or you'll think about it?'

'I'll think about it.'

Three times over the next few days she went to send an email to her father from Sebastian's address cancelling the dinner date. Three times she changed her mind. She distracted herself as best as possible. She visited the Art

Gallery, Federation Square, the museums. She went on a walking tour through the city centre's laneways and back streets.

She spent hours thinking about Jill's offer. She tried to picture herself in the role, meeting with potential clients, networking, interviewing staff. To get into the right mood, she changed into her most formal clothes: jacket, skirt, the dreaded work shoes. She put on her pearl earrings. Makeup. She sat in front of the mirror.

'Good morning. My name is Sylvie Devereaux. I'm the manager of the newly established Melbourne branch of Executive Stress Relief, the fastest growing recruitment agency in Australia. How may I help you?'

'Good afternoon. Thank you for coming to this presentation by Executive Stress Relief. My name is Sylvie Devereaux, manager of the Melbourne office, and I'm here to take the stress out of your staffing issues.'

'Thank you so much for our meeting, Mr Businessman. On behalf of Executive Stress Relief, I assure you I will do my utmost to provide you with professional and efficient staff-related services. Yes, despite our racy business name. And yes, I do insist you take your hand off my leg.'

She pulled a face into the mirror. 'For a good time, call Sylvie at Executive Stress Relief. Discretion assured.' Sebastian was right. It was a stupid name for a company.

She rang her mother. They talked about her painting, about the retreat, about Ray. Fidelma reported that Vanessa and Cleo had both decided to extend their holidays. Sylvie said she was enjoying Melbourne very much. She left it at that. She didn't mention her father or the job offer.

She had two messages from Max and Leila, inviting her to join them for dinner. Another night in a comedy club. She turned them down each time. Cupid didn't hang around after he shot his arrows either, did he? It was easier to think that than to give in to uncomfortable feelings of jealousy and disappointment.

The day before the dinner, she spent five minutes staring at her father's photograph. Was it too late? What would she say? What would he say? There was only one way to find out.

She texted Sebastian. Will meet Dad.

A one-word reply. Good.

Mill rang the afternoon of the dinner.

'Two quick tips, Sylvie. Coffee grounds make an excellent fertiliser for indoor plants. And a few drops of lemon juice will shine your shoes if you're out of polish. Now, tell me what's been happening with you in Melbourne.'

Sylvie told her about the dinner party, about the food,

about Donald having to leave. She also told her about Max and Leila. About Sebastian's matchmaking plans going awry.

'Good on you for trying something adventurous with the cooking,' Mill said. 'I used to love entertaining too. Vincent's friends would come over at the drop of a hat. Starving, usually. They'd eat for hours, then play for hours. The nights we had, I can't tell you. As for the business with the young man, perhaps it wasn't your turn with him. People go through seasons, I think. Like dogs. Perhaps your female friend and your male friend were in the right season for each other. That's the way it works sometimes. Another time, you and he might have been in the right season together.'

Sylvie laughed. Mill's words helped, in a strange way. 'Have you ever thought about writing an agony aunt column?'

'No, who'd listen to me? You just need to accept it and move on, Sylvie. What else can you do, try and split them up? Get him back? Too late for that. Let it run its course. If he was meant for you, he'll find a way back. Now, what else is going on?'

Sylvie said it before she realised. 'I'm having dinner with my father tonight.'

'Heavens above. Does your mother know?'

'No.'

'Don't tell her, for God's sake. She'll have kittens.'

Sylvie nearly laughed again. Her great-aunt had a way of defusing situations without realising. 'Mill, did you know him?'

'I met him a few times. And I was at their wedding, of course. What a grand affair that was.'

'What was he like back then?'

'Handsome. Talented. Absolutely mad about your mother in the early days.'

'Why did it go so wrong between them?'

'There were rumours, but whoever knows what goes on between two people.'

Sylvie didn't want discretion. 'What did you hear?'

Mill was quiet for a moment. 'I don't know what was gossip and what was truth. I heard talk of money worries. And Fidelma's a handful, of course. She always was, even as a child. An artist, you see. They're difficult. You should know, you've lived and worked with four of them, five, counting your father I suppose. I don't like those sisters of yours, by the way. Very stuck-up. Talented, yes. But extremely unlikeable.'

'They're artists. They behave differently. It comes with the territory. I know because I'm not artistic. I'm the boring one of the family. The square peg.'

'You are having a pity party today. Swimming in a sea of woe-is-me. Don't be silly. You can't have every-one in a family being an artist. And thank God for that. It would be an unworkable situation. Artists need support. They're helpless on their own. Painters, for example. They need gallery owners, framers, paint manufacturers. People to look at their work. Patrons. Look at Vincent van Gogh – helpless without his brother Theo. Musicians are the same, nothing on their own. I'm speaking from experience, of course. They need constant reassurance. Audiences. People to make their instruments. Build stages. Sell tickets. It's the same with writers. They need readers, booksellers, publishers, printers. Even comedians need people to laugh at their jokes. Try to look at it that way, Sylvie. Maybe your mother and your father and your sisters and your brother are the square pegs, the odd ones out. So needy. So fragile. In fact, I'd say they are. I've never met an artist who isn't odd, have you?'

'No.'

'Exactly. You're much better off being the person you are. Independent. Self-sufficient. Sane. Let them be the odd ones out and you can be the odd one in. Now, I must go. George is about to arrive and I promised I'd serve him a Harvey Wallbanger for cocktail hour tonight. Bye for now. Enjoy dinner with your father.'

CHAPTER TEN

Sylvie chose simple clothes. A pale-green T-shirt, a dark-green skirt. She put several sparkling clips in her hair, applied more makeup than usual, looked at herself for a long moment, then washed off the makeup and took out the clips. She wasn't glamorous like Vanessa or Cleo. There was no point pretending otherwise. If she disappointed him, there was little she could do.

Sebastian had been concerned about their father getting anxious. Sylvie's own blood pressure was heading sky-wards. This wasn't just a dinner. If she had been worried about life in Melbourne reaching childhood expectations, it had nothing on her expectations about her father.

She wanted to meet him. She needed to meet him. She was glad Sebastian had forced the issue. Because there was no way she would have dared do it herself. There was too much that could go wrong. She tried to keep perspective. They wouldn't run into each other's arms, like the scene in the final chapter of *The Railway Children* which always brought her to tears. Bobbie on the station platform, seeing her father for the first time in many hard months.

Sylvie knew the whole scene word for word.

'Oh! my Daddy, my Daddy!' That scream went like a knife into the heart of everyone in the train, and people put their heads out of the windows to see a tall pale man with lips set in a thin close line, and a little girl clinging to him with arms and legs, while his arms went tightly round her.'

Sylvie didn't know if she and her father would even touch each other. She could feel the young, hurt version of herself nestling deep inside still, the little girl who hadn't received any birthday cards, or phone calls, for many years. The same girl who had slowly and methodically sealed off the part of her mind that wanted to think about her father, who missed him. Who would like to have talked to him over the years.

Would they manage any of those conversations tonight? Manage to catch up on even one year of her life, let alone twenty-one? She wanted to, she realised. She looked in the mirror one more time before she left the apartment. 'Hello, Laurence,' she said to her reflection. 'I'm Sylvie, your daughter.'

She easily found the Malaysian restaurant. She had walked past it many times the last fortnight. There were about a dozen tables, half of them full. Before she had a chance to look around, the waitress came over and greeted her.

'A table for two, please,' Sylvie said.

'Do you have a booking?'

'I'm meeting someone.'

'Name?'

'Devereaux.'

The elderly man at the table by the window looked up. He was wearing a jumper that looked like it had seen better days. There was a jug of water in front of him. She looked closer. Curly hair. Enquiring eyes.

He said her name first. 'Sylvie?' He stood up. 'It's Sylvie?'

'Hello.' She stepped towards him. 'Sebastian couldn't make it. I came in his place.'

He was looking intently at her. 'I've seen photographs, of course, but they don't do you justice. You're lovely. You're like your grandmother.'

She gazed back at him. It was like time-lapse photography. The handsome man in the photos worn down by age, battered by life.

'Please, sit down,' he said.

There was so much to say she didn't know how to start. She watched him fidget with a napkin. All day she had rehearsed conversations in her head with him. Now her mind was blank.

He looked as uncomfortable as she was feeling. 'I'm sorry. I don't know where to start with chitchat.'

'I'm not good at chitchat either.'

He gave a brief smile. 'I've brought a couple of books. We could sit here and read if you like. Or I've got the crossword.'

It was a cryptic one, she noticed. 'Are you good at them?'

'Not bad.'

The waitress arrived with menus and a wine list. Two other groups of people arrived, taking tables behind and beside them. Sylvie felt very self-conscious. This hadn't been a good idea. A first meeting in twenty-one years in a public place like this?

Her father picked up the menu. She picked up hers. There was silence while they both read.

She looked up at the sound of a chair being pushed back. His chair.

He was standing up. 'Sylvie, I'm sorry. I can't stay.' His hands were shaking.

'But –'

'I'm sorry.'

She could only watch as he walked quickly across the room and out the door.

She sat for a few minutes. She couldn't follow him.

Wouldn't follow him. She politely told the waitress she needed more time.

'The gentleman?'

'He got called away.'

The second time the waitress came, Sylvie apologised and said unfortunately she needed to leave too. Her shock had turned to anger. As she walked out, the waitress gave her a puzzled look.

Sebastian rang her on her mobile before she had a chance to dial his number. 'Are you okay?'

'How do you know?'

'He rang me. From a phone box up the street, by the sound of things.'

Sylvie glanced around, expecting to see him. No sign. 'What the hell is going on, Seb? What games are you both playing with me?'

'Sylvie, it's not games, I promise you. I'm so sorry it's happened like this. But it's not something I think I should explain on the phone. Are you free tomorrow night?'

'Yes, but –'

'I'll ask for a night off. Come back to Melbourne and take you out to dinner. The same place. You'll like it. And you may even get to eat something this time.'

She knew he was trying to cheer her up, but it didn't feel funny. None of this did. She agreed on a meeting time, then abruptly finished the call.

She walked home, down Toorak Road, onto Punt Road, hardly noticing her surroundings. Was that it? That was her big reunion with her father? Their first conversation after all those years? She didn't know if she wanted to cry or rage or even laugh. She was completely confused. If anyone had the right to storm out, surely it was her? She was the one who had been abandoned.

She took out her phone again and pressed speed dial. She didn't waste time with a greeting. 'Seb, I need Dad's number. His address.'

'No, Sylvie. Not yet. After we've met.'

'Forget this. Stop trying to control me. You were at me because I didn't ask you for his details and now I want them you won't give them to me?'

'I made a mistake. I thought things would be different.'

'You thought he might stay long enough to have a glass of wine, you mean? A starter? A prawn cracker or two?' She took a ragged breath. 'What did I do wrong, Seb?'

'You didn't do anything. You couldn't have done anything.'

'What is it? You have to tell me.'

'Sylvie, I can't, not over the phone. It's a long story and I'm about to get called back to the set. It's not fair to you or him.'

'I'll go to the university tomorrow to see him, then.'

'He doesn't work there any more.'

'Then I'll go to his home. I'll look him up in the phone book.'

'He's not in the phone book.'

'Who is he? The Scarlet Pimpernel?'

'Sylvie, please. One more day. I'll be there tomorrow night. Before seven, I promise. Will you wait till then?'

It didn't look like she had any choice. 'Okay.'

'I'm sorry, Sylvie. I hoped it would be different. I made a big mistake.'

'It's not your mistake, Seb.'

'It's not yours, either. Remember that.'

There was no message from Mill waiting on the answering machine when she got home. There was, however, an email. Addressed to Sebastian, written to her.

Sylvie, I'm sorry. I hope Sebastian will explain things better than I can. LD

He hadn't even signed it Dad.

The next day stretched out too long and too lonely in front of her. She waited until nine and then phoned the other temp agencies she'd contacted. Whatever job was going, she'd take.

One hour later, she was in a boardroom on a fifteenth-floor office on Collins Street, surrounded by three thousand envelopes, address labels and circulars.

The young woman who'd met her at reception was apologetic. 'It's completely mindless work, I'm sorry. Just stuffing envelopes. I can get you a radio if you'd like one. And please take all the coffee breaks you need. You'll go crazy otherwise.'

'I'll be fine,' Sylvie said. 'It's perfect. Thanks very much.'

She was waiting in the restaurant when Sebastian arrived at ten to seven that night. He was carrying his bag and a laptop over his shoulder. He'd obviously come directly to the restaurant without going home first. It had been less than a fortnight since she'd seen him, but she nearly cried with the relief. He came straight over and gave her a hug.

'You okay, Sylvie?'

'Not really. How are you?'

'Work, good. Social life, good. Sister, worried about her. Brother, guilty he landed her in it.'

'What is it, Seb? Is he sick? Dying?'

'No quicker than any of us.' He glanced around for the waitress. 'Would you like a drink before we start? I'm presuming you didn't get a glass of wine with Dad last night?'

'He's an alcoholic. A drug addict. His life's a mess. That's what you're saying.'

'He's a mess, yes. But he's not an alcoholic. Or a drug addict. Not exactly.'

He wouldn't say more until they had ordered and a bottle of red wine was in front of them.

'Tell me everything, Seb. Don't leave anything out. Don't feel you have to protect me.'

'I don't any more.' He poured their wine. 'I'm driving you crazy waiting, I know, but I'm also proving a point. Good parts of life go on even when there are bad things in the background.'

'Nice philosophy but would you please just tell me?'

'Dad's a disaster area, Sylvie. Broke. Almost on the streets. He has been for years.'

She stared at him. 'You're making that up.'

He shook his head. 'He's got a gambling addiction. Not just an addiction. A curse. He's been ruined by it. He can't beat it.'

'Gambling? Horseracing? Poker?'

'Horses, dogs, cats probably. Cards. Sporting matches. You name it, he's gambled on it. He's been like it on and off all his life.'

'But how can he be a gambling addict? He's an academic. A poet.'

'That's got nothing to do with it. In any case, he hasn't worked at the university for sixteen years. He hasn't written poetry for years. Or if he has, he hasn't had anything published.'

Sylvie was having trouble taking it all in. 'Why didn't you tell me any of this before now?'

'He asked me not to. And I didn't want to. You felt bad enough about him as it was.'

'Then why didn't you tell me before I met him last night?'

'I should have, I know that now. But I didn't know what phase he'd be in. It's like alcoholism. He lasts weeks without gambling and then it's like a fever, it's all he does, all he thinks about, and bam, all the money's gone. He's been good the past few times I've seen him. I hoped he was still like that. That you'd get on okay, at least have a meal, a conversation with him before you learned about the whole situation. Did he have a jug of water in front of him when you arrived?'

Sylvie nodded.

'That means he's bad again. It's a kind of signal he has, to tell me I'll have to pay for dinner. If I arrive and he has a bottle of wine on the table, it's his shout. It's his way of telling me without telling me.'

'When did you find all this out? When you moved down here with him?'

He nodded. 'The giveaway was when the TV kept going missing. When the fridge stayed empty for weeks on end. When I realised if I wanted to study I'd have to find the fees myself.'

'But you never said anything. All those times you came up on visits. Why didn't you tell us? Tell me?'

'What was the point? Mum hated him anyway. Vanessa and Cleo had decided he was public enemy number one. And Mum wouldn't let you see him, in any case.' He paused. 'Do you wish I had told you before now?'

She thought about it. What would it have changed? She slowly shook her head. 'Seb, was it terrible? Has it been terrible for you all these years?'

'Sometimes, yes. Most of the time, it's sad but it's not terrible. It was harder for Mum than anyone, I think. You know he sold most of her family heirlooms before she realised what was going on?'

'The paintings? The lamps? That's where they went?'

He nodded. 'All sold to pay back debts. Nothing much has changed since then. He owns some clothes, a few books, that's about it. His house is practically a slum, as well, but it's the best he can do. He gets a pension these days, but it's touch and go sometimes.'

'So he's always been like this?'

'It was in his blood, I think. His father was a bookie, did you know that?'

Sylvie shook her head. She knew hardly anything about her father.

'Dad said it started with cards for him. Playing poker

with friends, games that turned into night-long sessions. Small bets that turned into big bets. From what he's told me, he was up to his neck in debts before he knew it.'

'And Mum always knew?'

'You don't remember them fighting about it?'

Sylvie remembered fights, but not what they'd been about. She'd always run to her room when they started shouting at each other.

'Any time they had any money, he spent it. Or took it. Mum had to kick him out or there would have been nothing left, I'm sure of it. I take my hat off to her. She's always been away with the fairies, but she did bring you all up. She's a shrewd businesswoman under all those silk scarves.'

'So after they divorced, Dad didn't help her financially?'

Sebastian laughed. 'Oh, he might have sent her the odd five dollar note now and then. When he wasn't on a poker binge or a greyhound binge or a horseracing binge.'

'But what about you, Seb? Who paid for your food and the rent and all of that?'

'I learned to steal too. Don't look so shocked. I stole from him. Out of his wallet, whenever I knew he had any money. I kept it hidden so we had enough to pay bills, buy food, cover the rent. Until I decided enough was enough and I moved out of there.'

'Did it make you hate him?'

Sebastian shook his head. 'He can't help it. No, that's not true. Sometimes he can and sometimes he can't. But put it this way, I learned at a young age never to say "Want to bet on it?" to him.'

They laughed a little at that.

'Is that why you moved out so young?' Sebastian had just turned eighteen when he got a flat on his own, she remembered.

'Part of the reason. I knew that if I stayed, I'd be forever bailing him out. I'd done enough of that. And that wasn't doing either of us any good. Especially after he lost his job. He kept skipping lectures to go to the bookies. It took a while, but eventually I realised it wasn't my job to take care of him.'

'Seb, I'm so sorry. I wish I'd known. For you, if not him.'

'I was okay, Sylvie. Really. I got mad sometimes, and then I'd get sad. It's the same now. But I still enjoy him. When he's in good form – pardon the racing pun – he's good company. He still reads a lot, still thinks. But I'm not in charge of his life, and he's not in charge of mine.'

'This is why he never got in contact with us, isn't it?'

'Most of the reason.' He was quiet for a moment. 'I've thought a lot about it, talked to people about it –'

'Therapy, you mean?'

'Nothing so interesting. I went to Gam-Anon. For

families of gamblers. I didn't like what I heard, but it made me understand there was nothing I could do about it. It suited Dad to live separately from me. It suited him to live separately from all of us. No Mum on his back, no kids to feel responsible for. Out of sight, out of mind, out of guilt.'

She felt tears well and blinked them away. 'I wanted to like him. I thought he would be the missing piece in my life. That meeting him would make everything right. And . . .'

Sebastian waited.

'I didn't feel anything. He was just an old man. An old man who got up and left in the middle of dinner.'

'Not even the middle. You didn't even get started, did you? Talk about a cheap date.'

She couldn't laugh. She was still too angry. Too hurt. 'What do I do now, Seb? Do I meet him again? Do I have to get to know him? Do I have to love him?'

'You have to do whatever feels right. But how can you love him yet? You don't know him.'

'He's my father. I'm supposed to love him, aren't I?'

'I don't think there are rules about that. If there are, he's broken a few of them. So I'd say you're even on that score.'

'Do you love him?'

'I like him. I feel sorry for him. I care what happens to him. Is that love? I don't know.'

During dinner Sebastian told her more stories of life with their father. Her eyes filled with tears again.

He noticed. 'Don't cry for me, Sylvie. Seriously. I still think I got the better end of the deal. You're the one who had to live with Fidelma and Heckle and Jeckle.'

'I wish I'd known. I wish I could have helped you.'

'There was no help to be done. And you know now.'

'Better late than never?'

'Exactly.'

Over coffee, she told him about the job offer from Jill. He was delighted for her. 'But you don't look too pleased.' He hesitated. 'It's not because of Dad being here in Melbourne, is it? Knowing about him? Has it ruined things?'

'No.' She thought about it. 'No, it hasn't. I'm still trying to work it all out. Whether I should take it. Where I would live. How I would live.'

'Of course you should take it. And the rest is simple. You'd live with me until you found your own place. My friends would be your friends. It's all here waiting for you, Sylvie. Your new life, waiting to be lived. Come on, get that sad look off your face. It's not the end of the world with Dad, I promise you. He's not the devil, or evil. He's just a mess. But it's his life, and he's living it the way he wants to. And we have to live our lives too.'

'I think I wanted a happy ending, Seb. I wanted it to all work out differently.'

'You're not at the end yet. Who knows how it will be between you? Give him some time. And give yourself some time as well. And try not to expect too much. He's only human. And so are you.'

'It's not that simple, is it?'

'I've had twenty years to think about it, Sylvie. It actually is that simple. Not easy, but simple.' He reached across and touched her hand. 'Trust me. I'm your big brother.'

Chapter Eleven

They left the restaurant straight after their meal. No visits to bars or late-night clubs. Sylvie helped Sebastian carry his bags up the stairs to his apartment. He was staying just the one night, returning to the film set the next morning.

'There'll be a message from Mill,' she said over her shoulder. 'She's started ringing each night with one of her handy household tips.'

'She has? I'm changing the number first thing tomorrow.'

The light was flashing. Sylvie smiled. 'Told you.' She pressed the button.

'Sylvie, it's Mill.' Her voice sounded odd. 'I need some help. I've a pain in my chest. I've rung my neighbours but they're out. I didn't want to make a fuss and ring the doctor but . . . it's a sharp pain. You're not there. I'll try –'

Sylvie exchanged an alarmed glance with Sebastian. She replayed the message.

'It's not a joke, is it?' Sebastian asked.

'She doesn't make those kinds of jokes.' Sylvie picked up the phone and rang Mill's number. There was no answer. She tried again. It rang out one more time.

She didn't hesitate. She dialled 000 and quickly explained.

'We can send someone around,' the operator said. 'What's the address?'

She didn't know. She'd never been to Vincent's house. 'It's a terrace in Surry Hills.'

'Miss, we can't help without an address. Can you find it out? Call us back?'

Sebastian rang Fidelma's number on the landline. He got the answering machine. Sylvie rang Cleo and Vanessa on their mobiles. She got their voicemail in both cases.

At Sylvie's suggestion, Sebastian logged onto the web and googled Vincent Langan's name. 'No good,' he called. 'It just says he lived in Surry Hills.'

Sylvie had a brainwave. 'Seb, quick, get the website for George's Gorgeous Gardens. He knows where she lives.'

George answered his mobile immediately. Sylvie urgently explained.

'I live just three streets away,' he said. 'I'll call the ambulance and go there right now myself. I've got a key.'

'Will you call me back?'

'As soon as I can.'

George rang back thirty minutes later. Mill was on her way to hospital. He'd found her unconscious on her living room floor. She'd had a heart attack.

'She's got a heart condition?'

'It's usually under control with tablets. But she's been so busy getting Vincent's house organised, she wasn't taking care of herself. But she'll be okay. She said it, the doctor said it. She also told me to give you a tip from her.'

'A tip? At a time like this?'

There was amusement in his voice. 'She said it was a simple one. "Never forget to take your medication."'

Sylvie awoke at seven the next morning. Sebastian was still asleep, his bedroom door shut. She dressed quietly and walked out into the misty morning.

She loved autumn in Melbourne. It felt different than it did in Sydney. She felt closer to nature, though it did help living next to the Botanic Gardens. She walked around the boundary of the gardens, listening to the traffic, the pounding feet of the joggers, snatches of conversation. She thought of the different parts of the city she had visited. All there was still to be uncovered.

The possibility of getting to know her father better, if he let her and if she decided she wanted to.

There were great opportunities for her, she could feel it. Different work, a new share-house, the distance she needed from her mother and sisters, the fun she would have with Sebastian. She got the feeling again. Of anticipation. Knowing she could take charge of her own life.

Sebastian was coming out of the bathroom in his dressing-gown when she let herself in.

'You've been to get me fresh croissants and orange juice. What a thoughtful sister.'

'I haven't but I can.'

'I don't eat breakfast. Make me coffee, though, and you'll be in my good books all day.'

She had a tray of coffee waiting on the table beside the bay window when he came back from getting dressed. She poured them both a coffee and then sat down opposite him.

'You look serious,' he said.

'I am.' It was the right thing to do. She knew it. 'Seb, I've decided something.'

'What?'

'I'm going back to Sydney. I was offered a job before I came down here. I'm going to take it.'

'What job? With the agency?'

She shook her head. 'As Mill's companion.'

He burst out laughing. 'That's a cracker, Sylvie. Bed-pans. Tablets. Oh yes, you'll be really happy.' He stopped and looked at her. 'Oh, my God. You're serious.'

She nodded.

'But what about the big Melbourne job?'

'I don't want it.'

'You'd be so good at it.'

'It's not what I want to do. I feel like I've done work like it already. Long hours. Stressful demands. It wouldn't feel new.'

'But Melbourne would be new. There's so much here.'

'I'll come down more often. See you more regularly.'

'It's not because of Dad, is it?'

'No.' She was sure of that. 'I wanted him to be different. I wanted him to want to get to know me. But that won't change whether I'm here or in Sydney, will it?'

Sebastian shook his head. 'No, I don't think so. But, Sylvie, talk about frying pan into fire. You're a young woman. Mill's an old, mad woman.'

'She's not. She's only in her seventies and she's not mad. Eccentric, but not mad. Did you know she was Vincent Langan's lover for forty years? That he was one of the best jazz musicians of his age? That what she doesn't know about household tips isn't worth know-ing? That she has lived through a world war? That she cooked dinner for every jazz and blues singer worth their note in Sydney in the fifties and sixties? She's full of stories. She's funny. I like her.'

'So ring her once a week. Become pen-pals. Why do you have to go and live with her?'

'I want to get to know her while there's still time. And she needs a hand getting her affairs in order.'

'More affairs? A woman of her age?'

'Her paperwork. She's got boxes of recipes and tips. All of Vincent's papers and his music collection. I'd like to help her with them.'

'You are serious, aren't you?' He laughed ruefully. 'Where did I go so terribly wrong?'

'You didn't go wrong. You went right. You showed me another way of living. A different way. And I realised this morning I liked the old way. I just needed to come at it from a different direction.'

'So you're moving back home?'

She shook her head. 'I'm moving into an upstairs room in Mill's house. It's painted blue and it looks out on a fig tree.'

'How do you know?'

'She told me.'

'But what if I said I want you to stay here with me?'

An echo. She thought of herself as a child. *I want to be with my brother.*

'If you still want me when we are old and grey, I'll

come and be your housekeeper. I just need to pick up all the tips from Mill first.'

'Not the racy ones. I don't want some slapper of a housekeeper living with me, bringing home elderly gents from the local bowls club.'

'I promise. No elderly gents.'

'Are you sure, Sylvie?'

'About the elderly gents? Yes, positive.'

'Not them.'

She smiled. 'I am sure, Seb. I'm absolutely sure.' She said it in a crisp English accent.

He grinned at her. 'Then come here and give your poor lonely brother a big hug. Your poor lonely abandoned brother.'

'That's emotional blackmail, isn't it?'

He leaned back and raised his eyes to the ceiling. 'She recognises it at last. My work here has not been in vain. Go forth, young Sylvie. You have my blessing.'

They hugged on it.

One week later, she had a farewell night out with Sebastian, Donald, Leila and Max. Dinner, drinks, lots of laughing. She was very aware of Leila and Max, still in the early stages of their relationship, all glances and touching. She felt pangs of regret, mixed up with jealousy, uncomfortable feelings. She made a conscious effort to seem relaxed and pleased for them both.

Sebastian was the life of the party, bemoaning the fact she was leaving, making fun of her. 'My plan went awry. I had it all sorted. Sylvie rents my spare room and cooks all my dinners, works part-time in Donald's bookshop and forms a long and lasting relationship with you, Max.'

Max shrugged, putting on a sad expression. 'She wasn't interested in me, I'm afraid. Obviously too used to those Flash Harry Sydney types. Still, I was able to drown my sorrows with Leila.'

'Stop that, you,' Leila said, with a too-loud giggle. 'Our meeting was fate and you know it.' She planted a big kiss on his cheek.

Sylvie kept a bright smile on her face, laughing with everyone else. Is that what Max had thought? That she hadn't shown any interest? Would everything have been different if she hadn't left the music club that night? Not taken offence at his curiosity about Vincent Langan? Would Leila still have knocked him off his feet? She was glad when Donald engaged her in conversation and she could turn away from Max and Leila.

The party ended soon after. Leila gave her a big farewell hug. 'I'll ring you, Sylvie. Every week, I promise. We can be long-distance friends.'

'I'd love that.' She meant it too.

Donald hugged her as well. 'Good luck, Sylvie. See you soon, I hope.'

'I hope so too,' she said.

Max was next. 'I hope Sydney treats you well. Keep in touch.'

'I will. You too.' She wondered if they would. She hugged him then pulled away first, for her own sake. He still felt good. Tall and solid. But out of her reach.

She arrived back in Sydney on the two thirty flight. She'd rung Fidelma and told her the news. Fidelma said it all sounded like a marvellous idea. She then told Sylvie about her plans for her new exhibition opening. Flame throwers, she was thinking, to tie in with the idea of the elements. Sylvie said she thought it sounded wonderful and gave her the name of two excellent event organisers. Fidelma didn't offer to collect her from the airport and Sylvie didn't ask. She was nearly thirty. She was perfectly capable of getting a taxi or a bus home. To her new home.

Mill had rung the night before to tell her once more how pleased she was at Sylvie's decision. She'd been out of the hospital for four days. She was fighting fit again, she said.

'We'll set some ground rules too, I promise. You're not coming to be my nurse. Or my companion, really, now I think about it. We can be partners. How does that sound?'

Sylvie thought it sounded good.

As she came out into the arrivals area, a man in his mid-thirties came up to her. Medium height, brown-faced, dressed in faded jeans and a long-sleeved T-shirt pushed up over muscled arms.

'Sylvie?' At her nod, he put out his hand. 'I'm George. Your aunt's gardener. She asked me to come and collect you.'

He had a smiling open face. She found herself smiling back at him. 'How did you know it was me?'

He picked up her case as if it was a matchbox. 'She said you were small and lovely. And you are. Come on, the car's this way.'

EPILOGUE

One year later

Sylvie and Mill were sitting on the swinging chair on the verandah, sipping from cocktail glasses. It had been a warm autumn day with sunshine and blue sky. Through the open French doors they could clearly see the TV set. On screen a bride and groom were dancing. The footage was shaky, as if filmed by an amateur. As the couple did a twirl, the husband tripped and went flying across the dance floor into the wedding cake. The footage ran forwards and backwards, all with a comical musical soundtrack.

The host appeared on screen, a backdrop of the groom with wedding cake all over him behind her. It was Leila. She put her hands on her hips and gave a big laugh. 'That's what I call trying to have your cake and eat it too! That's it for tonight. Please keep your videos coming in. Don't forget, if Calamity Calls, call me! Goodnight!'

As soon as the credits had rolled, Sylvie picked up the phone beside her and rang a Melbourne number. 'It was fantastic, congratulations.'

'You think?' Leila said. 'I've been hiding under the bed since I recorded it last week.'

'You're a natural.'

'What did Mill think?'

'Mill, what did you think?'

'A little ripper.'

Sylvie and Leila had kept in contact since Sylvie left Melbourne. Leila's career had got a sudden boost six months previously with her appearance on a fledgling comedy show on one of the community stations. A TV scout for one of the bigger networks had seen her. She was edgy and kooky, apparently. Just what he needed for the host of a new show of video bloopers from around the world. Each program would begin with a monologue from Leila telling about her latest catastrophe. She had no problem finding material, she told Sylvie.

Her relationship with Max had lasted only two months. A mutual decision. 'I'm not surprised,' Leila had said. 'Why should my love life be any less disastrous than the rest of my life? At least we're still on speaking terms. My last boyfriend nearly took out a contract on me.'

Leila had been up to stay with Sylvie and Mill twice.

She loved the house. 'It would make me want to take up jazz,' she said the first time. 'How long will the students get to stay here?'

'A year, but then we'll help them find other accommodation,' Sylvie explained.

Her sister Cleo had been disgusted. 'Wasting a beautiful house on scholarship students? Mill should sell it and move out into the suburbs. What a waste of money.'

'It was in Vincent's will,' Sylvie explained for the third time. 'He wanted Mill to use her inheritance to further jazz studies.'

'Couldn't she have bought a few CDs and given them to a university?'

'Vincent was from the country,' Mill had explained to Sylvie in her first week back in Sydney. 'He wanted me to do something to help other young musicians.'

It had been Sylvie's idea to turn the house into a home away from home for music students. Establish a trust that would continue long after Mill, or indeed Sylvie herself, had died. To also use Vincent's healthy royalties to fund three scholarships.

Vanessa was just as horrified. 'So you have to live with her and be her glorified secretary with no promise of a hefty inheritance at the end of it? You're mad.'

Twelve months earlier Sylvie had known nothing about jazz, or composing, or the difficulties young musicians faced. Now, she couldn't say she was an expert, but she was definitely a fan. The house was filled with music, talk of music, music magazines. At the moment, there were three students living with her and Mill. A piano player from the Hunter Valley, a trumpet player from Alice Springs and a double bass player from Perth.

There were great plans for the future, too. Open days twice a year, so visitors could stroll through the house, learn about Vincent's career, look at original sheet music, hear old recordings and read about the jazz scene in Sydney from the late 1950s onwards.

Sylvie was busy five days a week. Every day was different. Mill was the ideas person, but she left most of the work to Sylvie. It worked best that way, they'd discovered. And lately, Mill had been otherwise occupied.

Sylvie had dropped a collection of her tips into the local free newspaper. Since then, Mill had been contributing a fortnightly 'Ask Mill' column. She read each letter that was sent in and spent some time drafting her replies. The questions had been about cooking and housekeeping to begin with. These days, most of the hundred or so letters she received each week were about relationship problems. A producer from one of the radio stations who lived locally had read several of the columns and invited Mill on to his show. She had unfortunately sworn in the first broadcast, but once the fuss died down (there'd been twenty calls of complaint, apparently), he hoped to bring her back for another show.

'He'd better hurry up before I die,' was all Mill said about it.

In Melbourne, Sebastian and Donald were still together, still happy. She heard snippets of news about Max from Sebastian. He wasn't working in the book-shop any more. He had been offered work with a touring comedy production. It had come to Sydney but Sylvie had been away with Fidelma at the retreat that week. She went away with her mother every few months. It always coincided with Ray's visits to see his children from a previous marriage. Sylvie preferred it that way.

She sent the occasional email to her father. He sent the occasional one back. So far they had written only about books they'd read and films they'd seen. Each sentence seemed heavy with other meaning, but Sylvie didn't know where to start and didn't know if her father wanted her to. Fidelma still hadn't asked about him. Sylvie hadn't mentioned him either. She had reached no firm decisions or conclusions about him, or her feelings for him. She was taking Sebastian's advice, going slowly and letting it unfold in a way they both could cope with. No happy ending, but the best they could do.

'So have you seen Max yet?' Leila asked now on the phone.

'Max? Seen him where?'

'There. He's in Sydney. He got a one-year contract with the Sydney Theatre Company. I gave him your number last month. We caught up for a drink before he left. He said he was going to call.'

'No, he hasn't.' The sudden pang surprised her.

'I've got his number if you want it.'

'Sure,' she said, sounding as casual as she could, while her heart started beating faster. She took down the number.

Beside her Mill was making a show of looking at her watch. They were due over at Gorgeous George's house for dinner. It was apparently to celebrate his third child's fifth birthday, but Sylvie knew it was any excuse for a party. George and his wife Sarah had become Sylvie's good friends in the past twelve months. They had hit it off immediately, from the moment George picked her up at the airport.

She said a quick goodbye and another congratulations to Leila, then hung up. Mill had her eyes shut, head leaning back against the verandah rail, the near-empty cocktail glass in her hand. Mill was taking lots of catnaps these days. Not surprising, she was seventy-four years old. And working hard for a woman of her age.

'Mill?' Sylvie asked.

'Mmm?'

'There hasn't been a call for me recently that you forgot to pass on, has there?'

'Man or woman? Friend or foe? Family or non-family?'

'Man. Friend. Non-family. Called Max.'

'Now I think of it, yes. Last week.'

'What did he say?'

'Asked to speak to you.'

'What did you say?'

'Said you weren't home.'

'Was I?'

'Nope.'

'Did you forget to tell me or decide not to tell me?'

'It never hurts a man to have to do a bit of running after his prey.'

'I'm not Max's prey and you know it's rude not to pass on messages.'

'You've got his number now, haven't you?'

'Were you eavesdropping then?'

'Of course. That's why I got the hearing aid installed. So I could hear.'

They took simultaneous sips from their cocktail glasses.

'Mill, can I ask for a tip?'

'Ask away.'

'If you had met someone and thought that something might happen between you but before it did, something happened to make it impossible, but then it looked like you had a chance to make something happen, what would you do?'

'I'd ring him,' Mill said. 'Declare your intentions. Show your interest. As soon as possible.'

'Now, you mean?'

'Now,' Mill said. 'Before we go to Gorgeous George's.'

Sylvie went inside to make the call. He answered on the fifth ring.

'Max?'

'Sylvie?'

This time she didn't want to make a mess of it. She wanted to be clear. 'Max, I'm sorry to launch into it even before we catch up on each other's news, but can I please ask you three questions?'

'Of course.'

'Are you seeing anyone at the moment?'

'No, I'm not.'

'Do you still hold a candle for Leila?'

'No, I don't.'

'Would you come on a date with me one night? A proper date?'

She could hear the smile in his voice as he answered.

'I'd love to, Sylvie.'

She came back out to Mill. 'He said yes.'

'Of course he did.'

'What do you mean "of course he did"?'

'I told him when he rang last week that if he messed you around again, I'd kill him.'

'You didn't.'

'I did. That's what families are for, isn't it? To look out for each other? Now, hurry up or we'll be late.'

Also by
MONICA McINERNEY

Family Baggage

Tour guide Harriet Turner knows all about journeys. She's arranged hundreds of them for the travel agency her family runs. But nothing has prepared her for the drama, the hilarity or the passion of the *Willoughby* tour . . .

When her foster sister Lara vanishes suddenly, Harriet is left in charge of a party of tourists on a theme tour of Devon and Cornwall. The eccentric group are fans of *Willoughby*, an English TV detective show, and can't wait to meet Patrick Shawcross, the handsome actor who played him fifteen years ago.

For Harriet, the tour turns into a different kind of journey – a journey of self-discovery. She finds herself confronting questions about her family, her childhood, and her powerful feelings for Patrick Shawcross.

And the most puzzling question of all: where is Lara?

'This is one of those rare books you could recommend
to anyone and know that they'll love it'
Australian Women's Weekly

'A book to treasure that is clever, amusing
and heart-warmingly touching'
Woman's Day

The Alphabet Sisters

Sisters are always there for each other – aren't they?

Anna, Bett and Carrie Quinlan were childhood singing stars – the Alphabet Sisters. As adults they haven't spoken for years. Not since Bett's fiancé left her for another sister...

Now Lola, their larger-than-life grandmother, summons them home for a birthday extravaganza and a surprise announcement. But just as the rifts begin to close, the Alphabet Sisters face a test none of them ever imagined.

An unforgettable story of three women who learn that being true to themselves means being true to each other.

'You'll be laughing out loud one minute and crying the next'
Cosmopolitan

'A gentle and life-affirming story. We come away feeling better about the world and, maybe, just a little more tender towards those close to us'
Sydney Morning Herald

Spin the Bottle

Lainey Byrne is a woman in control, juggling a hectic job, her boyfriend Adam and a family with more than its fair share of dramas.

Things go into a spin when she is wrenched from her life in Melbourne to run a B&B in Ireland for a year. Bed-and-breakfast quickly tumbles into bed-and-bedlam, especially when a reunion with childhood friend Rohan Hartigan sparks an unexpected dilemma.

Meanwhile, back in Australia, her father's taken to his bed, her mother's up the walls, her three brothers are running amok – and as for Adam . . .

It's going to take more than a game of spin the bottle to sort this one out!

'A cosy, light-hearted romp, highly recommended'
Australian Women's Weekly

'As fresh, funny and engaging as its popular precursors,
A Taste for It and *Upside Down Inside Out* . . . This is
comfort reading – warm-buttered toast with
Irish honey spread right to the crusts'
Adelaide Advertiser

Upside Down Inside Out

Ever been tempted to pretend you were someone exotic, someone adventurous . . . someone different?

Set in Ireland, England and Australia, this is the funny and heartwarming story of two people whose lives are about to turn upside down and inside out.

Eva is off to Australia on a break from her job in a Dublin delicatessen, hoping to forget a fizzled romance and find inspiration for a new career. Joseph is taking a holiday from his stressful London job.

Each is on a search for some answers about life. Then something quite unexpected happens.

They meet each other.

'Sparkling . . . it's all systems go for a wonderful romance . . .
A long, glorious romp with a supporting cast of entertaining characters. The author leads us skilfully through this maze of near-misses and misunderstandings, and delivers a charming story told with large doses of love and humour'
Australian Women's Weekly

'An effervescent blend of romance, humour, travel and adventure'
Marie Claire

A Taste for It

Maura Carmody's off on the trip of a lifetime. A talented chef, she's travelling around Ireland for a month to promote Australian food and wine.

She's expecting a straightforward business trip. But what she gets is a whirlwind of mishaps, misunderstandings, rivals and revelations – and Dominic Hanrahan, who's giving her *plenty* of food for thought.

Set in Ireland and Australia, *A Taste for It* is a warm, funny novel about following your heart and pursuing your dreams.

'It takes only a minute or so before Monica McInerney's take on the world has you laughing. A feelgood funny story . . . romantic comedy at its best'
West Australian

'Effervescent . . . overflows with good humour and laughter'
Sydney Morning Herald